BECOMING A STAR IN YOUR GHETTO

2020

ALSO BY Y.V. RENE:

My Secret Love.

The Polygamist.

Becoming a Star in Your Ghetto.

Love with the Village Girl.

Why You

…And religious books.

VESOHGAH RENE

BECOMING A STAR IN YOUR GHETTO

BECOMING A STAR IN YOUR GHETTO

Prologue

Siesta!

On my hoary murky vetoed double-seat sofa, void of exquisiteness for its oldness; the material torn all over – on the dirty lone precluded double-seat settee – my head reposed on its arm, as my body sunk in between its woods, I lay.

On my back, my body depended on the couch, as my face stationed at the old roof of the rejected village plank cottage. Apprehending the cobwebs snugged here-and-there in the bungalow, my eyes labored. Through the gloom my face toured in a jiffy, landing on my few outfits hanged on a black cord tight at the wall – it's a blue, turn by dirt to a black rope. My eyes raced within an instant, I perceived people chatting, and youngsters frolicking outside – through the fissures between the plank walls. Clatters from prattles and hilarities diversified, as an intense nauseating pong hovered through the walls and landing on me. As usual, my mind said. Natures warbled their habitual 'good afternoon songs,' from the backyard.

It's noon!

Struck with grogginess, I relaxed, as my neck began unleashing a plodding antagonistic awkwardness, it rose. Thoughts cruised athwart my cognizance. I inaugurated a craving for an improved life; this chair in this dump is not where you were meant to be, my mind told me. Moreover, there's a lot life can bid to one like you, my contemplations persisted. How was I?

A longing for a respectable today struck me austerely, as my cognizance anticipated boulevards and routes that couldn't be probable if face to. Anger towards none obsessed my heart, as my face divulged. Furious on my bed, – the dirty old rejected double-seat couch was my bed – my mind unrelenting in nuisances. A shroud soared to my assessment; I inaugurated valuations at things from a deferent facet.

A subterranean confidential detonated in my observance, as I began to reason not like in some minutes back. I was absolutely in an altered world. I could fancy the appellation of this outlandish realm. I reminisce myself calling it, 'a world of all possibilities.' It was indeed a world where any could thrive in his soul-anticipated dreams. For sure, it was a world where none was indorsed to lay culpabilities on any.

Still in this new world of mine, my mind hefty with queries uncanvassed. My mouth through my lips drizzly, with philosophies to counter down. My eyes in a bombshell, like a virgin in her first night. My core hoarded with oodles to be divested. Blur in the trance of a cavernous rhema of occurrences, I began to clutch some certain things regarding life.

Concealed solely in the corporeal by this bizarre new-world of views, I started talking and acting like one from there. The plays and chatters began to fissure into some inaudible thuds, abetting the atmosphere to be soother. A profound trance in which I was filled with serenity congested my mind. Life began to be flawless, as I engrossed on my contiguous. Ideas on how to qualify the physical world cruised athwart my cognizance. Names on how this world could be referred to whack my wits, cripplingly. The world wasn't far from a ghetto!

The dark sky!

Fastening my eyes up, I saw the sky. It's night, my mind articulated. And you're outside, I hummed inaudibly. Still beholding the dark sky while installed at my veranda, thoughts of the afternoon scenarios of my poor hoary roof while on my dirty rejected old couch, sailed across my mind. My eyes retained up, sundry contemplations, my mind travailed.

The dark sky isn't far from a ghetto!

Flipping my eyes to and fro, probing what I couldn't explicate. Too many stars but the sky is still dark, my mind said. I could see so many stars, but not ample light to eradicate the darkness from the sky. Minutes passed through to hours, still on the same spot. I relished the world of thoughts.

In a jiffy, I saw myself as one of the stars. Lessons and questions I couldn't probed while afar, began coming flawless to my assessment. The afternoon feelings while on my dull stale vetoed divan began to be invigorated in my insinuations.

Same contemplations emanated to my mind, as I stared at the sky. Flabbergasted at their shinning knack, capacious things I noted. 1All the stars where shinning, my mind said. And that was the first thing I noted. And the second, 2the sky is very dark…

From there, as nature is encoded to function by chrono – the Greek word for 'time' – which is made of seconds, minutes, hours etc. I had to rest. The dark sky wasn't far from a ghetto.

Restaurant!

On my way to the native restaurant nearby, at the village square. It's 9am and you have to be fast, I told myself. I had to be quick because the food uses to get finished by 9:30am. Normally, the woman doesn't usually prepare much, for limited where the clients. So she always cooks little quantity for the few interested, and I was among.

"Give me corn and beans for 150Frs." I told this black-fat-woman, garbed in a robe, locally known as kabba in the area – it's an African loose-fitting robe, mostly worn by pregnant women. Though she wasn't.

Sitting on one of the benches, I observed her as she hassled with fanaticism to serve me. Ready to eat, my craving careened through my esophagus edgily, and equipped to condense the food scrumptiously.

Our localities aren't different from a ghetto!

As she was dishing the food, I could grasp the phantasmagorias of yesterday's experience with my old cobwebbed roof, as the stars in the night reemerged to my view. Around the plank housed restaurant, where other slat houses. Many sat next to me, for the same food. Maybe because it's less costly, I reasoned, enthralled on my stomach.

"Give my change." I said, elongating five-hundred-francs note to her, expecting three-hundred-and-fifty-francs for my balance, after the breakfast. That'll be till dinner.

Not gratified by what I'm beholding around, my soul mourned, as I paced back to the house. Still in this innovative world of mine, my mind inflates, as I tacit the arcane. I called it personal revelation. Inaudibly stirring towards my local cottage, with my old dirty rejected double-seat couch as my bed, to digest the food during siesta.

Oh! It's 4pm, my mind screamed.

In alacrity, I raised my head from the arm of the old rejected dirty double-seat couch, on which I was laid. I have to go for prayers by 4:30pm, I prompted myself. I have just less than 30minutes to get myself ready, which wasn't an issue.

Arranging myself, I left for prayers. The church is at Batoke, from Bakingili to Batoke is just some few kilometers. Taking a taxi will make it easier.

Back from prayers.

On my dirty old rejected double-seat couch, I napped. Trying to analyze the day's schedule. Just back from the church, I am tired. Blinking my reminiscence on the busyness of those I encountered in the day, I couldn't miss my usual position on the veranda at 7pm, meanwhile it was time. I will need to stretch myself outside. Our localities aren't different from a ghetto.

Watching the dark sky for a while, I could see it as our societies. How dark the world is, and concealed by torpors as my dirty old rejected roof.

The same thing that discrete my imagination the last night, emanated to my awareness. The stars, I thought. What sorts the variance is the stars. From here I began seeing how our various ghettoes needs numerous stars for its buoyant magnificence.

Answers were progressively impending to my queries. There's no answer without a question, as there's no query without a response. But what crafts the alteration is that the answer is part of the question, as the autopsy is a flake of the riposte. The response is in the question, and the query is in the answer.

So it is with glitches. There's no problem without a solution, as there's no elucidation deprived of a knotty. The solution is in the problem. The wants others are having is the response for you aiding them through. Because there's ample today, shows that there won't be tomorrow. The existence of one gives birth to the presence of the oncoming. All the answers to my questions about this ghetto called life was all revealed to me. Then, inscription was the best thing, to pass it on…

It was the afternoon of March 15 2018, and I was in Bakingili, a village in Limbe II Subdivision, Fako division of the southwest region of Cameroon. Being there as a proselytizer, this engrossment fetched a gargantuan alteration in me, by gifting me with tenacity and a tang to life. Then I pledged myself to postmortem the stars and their utilities, which I did. And I'm here to warrant it on…

The "*" sign indicates the statement from each star…

ONE

GHETTO AND FUNCTIONS

Fathoming the mysteries am seeing. My mind began yearning, as she waited for the totality of what she felt, regarding creation. The zephyr of acumen appeared substantial than what none could fancy. The squall of awareness wafted through the twitches to the comprehensive incredulity of my wits paramount anticipations on what this ghetto paraphernalia could be. Sited on the old tattered arm of my rejected bed, was my head, bursting with speculation, as she procured profound contemplations on what this whole fiasco as any would call, could be.

Ghetto and functions!

Still in the new world of mine. Vague from the physical contemporaneous, my mind static into the prodigious cosmos of new thoughts about these ghettoes. A sagacity of what it was, began probing my carcasses, as my skull became malleable, welcoming his attendance with joy. I began exuding beams of serenity, as a man oozing out his nous of predilection into the woman of his hallucinations within the few minutes of his very first time.

A ghetto!

As I envisaged, the appellation sounded primeval and sacrilegious to my cognizance, through to the auricles of my verdicts. But I reckoned it veracious shelving it the way it came. Compelling things the way they are, is the ethical syntheses to its sum. The archaic encyclopedic of the name was flamboyant to the extern I couldn't halt converging to discern what it was.

The appellation may sound antiquated to your earshot. But I took it the way it came in other not to be unattached from the context. Then my mind pontificated me on the term…

My first lectures.

"You may've censored the connotation, maybe because you're monotonous to the term in your day-today live. Most especially as an African, and others from other parts of the globe. Above all, the denotation is not at all floated off the gen of what it means…

…Thus several may abide the lexicon elucidation of what a ghetto is, but for contingent understanding, a ghetto is, 'the uncivilized chunks in which the curtailed class of both the educated and the amateur populaces who are not suitable to drudgery like others for a healthier grossing, to caucus a living for their dreams and anticipations in life has found billeted for themselves. There, they live with the notions that lone the fittest subsists.' Nevertheless, several will deliberate on the issue." He stated.

I was concerted to procure ancillary of the syrupy lessons. Just the delineation retained an opaque groundwork on which I could digit other stuffs. As he vouchsafed in me a pending for auxiliary delineation, my head was laid serenely on the old dirty rejected couch of a bed, where my body sunk in-between its woods.

Minutes later, he unremitted with the soothing homilies. "It's imperative you apprehend what a ghetto is, since the pivotal point is to grasp what it is, before reuniting how one can convert into a triumph in it. Several are those in their ghettoes shorn of sanguinities in ensuing in anything in life". He said, sounding dexterous.

Tranquil, on my old dirty rejected double-seat couch, with my head laid on it arm. My cognizance fetched bygone reminiscences of physical idiosyncrasies I've had with folks of altered sorts on their voyage of the analogous life. Flipping through their experiences as shared with me. The folios of foiling appeared to be auxiliary than that of triumph stratums.

Life acrimonious to my mandibles, my mind toured, as I perceived an identical ditty from all. On the same journey, I've grasped several folks and communed with most of them, but the same story. I could clutch the various ghettoes embryonic before me. Was it the same with the stars? I speculated. Moreover, it wasn't nocturnal yet, for me to probe the stars. Disconcerting my mind in thoughts, the folios of scrutiny I had with people emanated to my wits.

The unabridged enchilada elicited me; I was only 20 years old. A fledgling missionary, inquisitive to ascertain the surreptitious to true attainment in glee. It was certainly an advantage that I wouldn't afford to gaffe. From his word I was a bit conceptually heaving, then I probed, "Can you please talk about yourself sir?" for I craved to discern his supplementary. Hearing the perspicacity he carried, I hankered to be acquainted with him.

Then he continued. "I've been jammy to dialog with sundry about their lives, and several are those who've given-up on life. That you haven't bourgeon yet doesn't indicate unfeasibility, but because you haven't tacit how to thrive in your yearnings. When you twig how to proliferate in your anticipated dreams, feat will be contiguous to your clutch. Just grasp your ghetto (sky). You will know more about me as we continue." He said.

Then I intervallic, perceiving that he doesn't like interlude while chatting, I needed to elucidate a scrunch. At least, questions are not unscrupulous. "Sir, you mentioned 'ghetto', and you attached it to the 'sky'. I don't understand it sir." I probed. He grinned; he was ready to convers on it.

Then he said, "It appears you have oodles of questions…" He was alacritous to riposte. "One of the reasons why many haven't tacit this is because they don't know that their ghettoes should be their foci for attainment in life, which they should hanker for. Your ghetto is not partial to the delineations obtainable. Your ghetto is where you're most blissful in, or where you never hypothetical. A ghetto to one may not be a ghetto to another. The motive why it's a ghetto to you, is because it entails your star to darn. Let authenticity demeanor your assessment. One may not vanquish something big if he/she can't see a substantial prerequisite. How you see the requisite entails your quota for feats. Everyone has a ghetto because all were born for an alteration therein. Most people don't know that they have ghettoes waiting for their stars. Until you grasp your ghetto, you may never pleat something gigantic for the aid of those there." He elucidated.

I was like napping, but my eyes where wide uncluttered. I was copiously conceded away by the syrupy lessons. Then he gratified my sentience, telling me that he had a diminutive counsel for me.

Then he told me, "Precincts have wrought the manner in which many are seeing things today. The world at its globe is a ghetto, that in her day-to-day live, she necessitates vicissitudes."

Scrutinizing this, I conveyed it in itinerary with this world, and back to veracities in this my spanking realm. My mind hoisted in my acumens hemmed in my cranium that snoozed on the armrest of the dirty old rejected double-seat couch, in the dirty old rejected village plank bungalow. My eyes where open, but I couldn't twig anything abstract.

Hours passed, and half a day. I wasn't any longer in the corporeal. Food wasn't my worry, for my last cash was disbursed in the taxi. The sentimentalities were more delicious than Ndolee – local traditional food. But there was a problem. As this deliberations and orthodox revelations cruised passed my mind, a query whack my wits through to my core. What's a ghetto? I probed myself.

Stringency upsurge from my nadirs, as sanguinities were invigorated in my cubicles. Stimulated from my depths, I coveted to question my new dynamic elusive tutor. I knew that these will procure in me an enormous alteration. In my ambiguous shabby cottage of no light, my beams could be grasped on my face, as it curled my orifices.

I could comprehend the flares of the negativities of life. But I would fissure for his riposte, for I was going to ask. I beheld the infantile queries I grew up with. My enquiries of why was I born here, an Africa, etc. were tenaciously impending to my unabridged assessment. The queries on why is there subornment, sleaze, burglary, redundancy, and why God not assassinating the devil, etc. were all the ovaries of my cognizance. Tenacity was about to be born in me. I couldn't wait to ask him more…

I was a bit blur here. I necessitated elucidation. This ghetto paraphernalia was becoming a psychosis in my cerebral. I needed to ascertain what these ghetto homilies was all about, and then I probed, "But Sir, what is a ghetto?" I needed a knot share of what 'ghetto' was.

What the Ghetto is …

I was so ecstatic for he was alacritous to riposte me.

Then he articulated, "There's none bereft of a ghetto. Don't ruminate that folks at the metropolitan constituencies, born in amenity; and the salaried, mollified in life, doesn't necessitate the ghetto…

…Your ghetto is that chunk in which the exhibition of your flair and skills are required to be unembellished for those there to smile. There's an occupancy where your star is looked-for. You're not born to ubiquitous, but permeating in the place, your ghetto. Most are those that catches preference in peripatetic ubiquitously, who culminates not gratifying their cravings, because they flop to insinuate their ghettoes with the prerequisites therein. Your ghetto will recompense you supplementary than your congenial cruises in the world, if you comprehend it and the necessities therein." He told me. Very profound and flawless, the delineation was.

My hush signposted to him that I craved supplementary of his sermons…

"Your ghetto entails your presence to lionize you into becoming a star that the world will see and emulate. Devoid of your ghetto, you cannot breed spiraling. One of the reasons why there're ghettoes is because there are unrealized stars in the world. You might not have been jammy to be born in your ghetto, but the essential to annotate is that, each is innate for his or her ghetto, locate yours. You may have come from the luxury, and your ghetto is found in the colliery, and vice versa. Unearth yours for it entreaties your star to brand it sheen. If you're not executing the veracious thing in your ghetto, you may not glow in life."

From here, I could grasp the entirety because I was use to the dark sky, and the shining stars at night. Then he continued…

"Unless you portray the overseas you so love, as a ghetto that needs your star, you may not bloom there. Even if all the decorum on earth were endorsed to you, it will be like a privileged chump. The foreign great countries are not paradise, in which you enter to relish virtuous tithing for naught, rehash your assessment of it, and start seeing it as a ghetto that requests your star to linger reigning. Then you'll flourish there deprived of ample exertions. Anywhere you can depict as a ghetto, your feat is there if you've grasped your star." He told me.

The conundrums were so prodigious to me. I couldn't afford to omission any of his librettos. He was unswervingly admonishing me. I began intuiting bumpy as he pontificated to me. That was good though. Since he was my tutor, I was certain to trail all his articulates.

Then he asked me, "What is your own star in your ghetto?" I was misplaced as I lay unobtrusively. Then he continued…

"Your assessment towards the world delineates your methodology, and the manner she'll clutch you. Seeing the world as a boss that has everything, loiter you as a servant, to marmalade remunerations from her. Altering the world, should be your panorama, and how to do that, your exposé. Eyesight your ghetto, in other to be perceived (shine). Your constituent chunk of sight for alteration is your ghetto. That you haven't corroborated yet doesn't denotes that you don't have it…

…You may've been born in sumptuous, instigating that you were innate to merry and culminate in your luxurious stage, shouldn't be! Rifle your ghetto, for it can be aloof from superfluity. You may have a ghetto that prerequisite intuiting your comfy fluency. Your star crave to gleam, your star should glow for you were born for that resolve. Grasp your ghetto and pace towards that. She isn't a quiescent abode, but that of toil. You'll ascertain armistice, bliss and factual serenity lone in your ghetto." He halted.

I was ascertaining what my unabridged eons on earth couldn't worth. Then he told me where the ghetto is, in a knot share.

"From these lessons, I think you can fissure where this ghetto is. Nonetheless, the world at its orb is a global ghetto, assess your department." He rounded up. Still on my old dirty rejected double-seat couch. I was exhausted. Receiving these oodles of stuffs, I was so exhilarated.

It's evening!

On my old dirty rejected couch of a bed, I'm bushed. Taking a promenade to the village square will aid me. "I salute bro!" I greeted one of my neighbors at the road side. I'm on my way to have food on credit, with the old debt, I don't know if she'll consent today. She's my costumer. Am on my trail to prominence through my new-found tutor I ramble with, diurnally.

Outlining the cheaper site, I could get my favorites, Fufu and Eru – a local dish. Though cheap, I love it, I'm used to it. Ample steps auxiliary on foot, music booming. "Music always." I intoned, in the intense hubbub, none could perceive my voice. The volume was tremendously graded. Yeah, in Cameroon there's autonomy in anything music. There's no maximum to which the volume is rated. All can play to the utmost melodies.

Dusk in the area has to be the lone time for the inhabitants to lurch about, though the ghost-town has decelerated activities. Several are vending food and other stuffs in the twilight. I wouldn't go to any other place, for others won't assent, since cash wasn't in attendance.

Going for the one she'll easily give out for credit is the sagest insinuation, I went for.

Cameroon, an acreage heterogeneous with diverse ethnic groups and ethos. The multiplicity in indigenous foods diverges to each ethnic. I wouldn't afford to eat something insubstantial, for the day was vigorous. Fufu and Eru will be the superlative meal for me.

Back home, I slept.

The next day!

"Good morning!" I greeted my neighbor, as I winged my door on its creeps, in the morning. I couldn't articulate how the night was, for I hadn't any good night before. So I couldn't tell a bad night from the good. But thanks to the nature I'm awake, and ready for the day.

The exhilaration from yesterday's familiarity has augmented my fondness for my village cottage and my dirty old rejected double-seat couch. Elongating myself on the old dirty rejected bed, my pioneering realm was unwrapped before me for supplementary exhuming. Invigorating my cognizance on prior lessons, I grinned.

My core hankered, as my mien kinky in woe. My maws tautened, and my tongue tasted syrupy. My sentience slackened, as this query perforated my cognizance. Where is this ghetto? The question. I will need to arcade it down for his ripostes, since he was constantly there. Life bequeathing books to me, I couldn't recite. Beholding at nature, she seemed biased. Benevolent to myself, I crestfallen my observance. I could grasp specimens gazing at me, profound in my mien.

From here I craved to simplify myself on an opinion that I conceded for years, leading me protractedly. I incarcerated it so taut. It was a concept somebody passed on to me. Then I probed, "Please sir, there's this question I wish to ask." I said, perceiving that he was alacritous to response, though still early. I progressed to the question. "I once heard a man said, 'not all were created stars,' and another said, 'when your neighbor is more than you, you should hold his bag and walk behind him.'" I ended.

Eavesdropping at him acutely, he said, "I don't go laterally with that, why? Because all are stars in their various constituencies. You'll become a pouch-container only when you gaffe to pace in route with your department. There's not a soul shorn of a prospective in life, (a sole miniature or disproportionate propensity about one thing or another). The world is a ghetto; we all are in the ghetto. The universal ghetto is alienated into trifling ghettoes. Your meadow of assessment is your unit in the global ghetto."

Then he used a quotation, as I wrote it down instantaneously, on a piece of carton, since there wasn't a piece of paper, I couldn't afford one. Here's the quote. The way he said:

Quote… We may be looking at the same direction, but not seeing the same thing; what you see from the same direction we are looking at, may be different from what I see…

Perceiving that I was illogical on the focus, from his guise, I discerned that he wanted to break it down for an improved understanding for me.

Then he said. "Don't halt observing an unambiguous terminus because copious once looked at it, or because somebody is still beholding it. Your assessments can be divergent. That you looked at the path and botched, doesn't exhibit that if I gaze at it, I'll flop. Our opinions are dissimilar. One can be observing at an explicit trajectory, because he sees it striking, and another because he want to swot, and you, because you want to alter it. Note that many have been gazing at that same direction, and it has still remained the same. Stares don't transmute, but assessments do. Your ghetto requires you and not someone else, that's why it's 'your ghetto.' The reason for the world' motionless stage is because we ruminate that one can function in another's ghetto and still better the world…He halted, noticing as I shuddered my cranium in grins. I knew that he was exhilarated having me obtains the teachings.

Then he continued. "…You may not bud in your ghetto with off-beam drives. You want the world to be an enhanced domicile and brand you a star, while your foremost ambition for work is to make your family blissful. This alone is an impeccable motive that your ghetto won't be gratified with you about. For you to know your ghetto forthrightly, you need to prolix veracious motives. Let your stance be about how to enhance the world through your star. If you can't see the global ghetto, then you won't be proficient to handle your minor ghetto and the necessities therein. Your ghetto is situating where you've clutched the need for your presence and flair." He ended.

On my antediluvian couch, I ruminated profoundly. In my pursuit to ascertain the remits of life. Perspicacity was assimilated in its synopsis, I discerned. But being the drupes of mind to several, I trailed to drill it for physical fallouts. My eyes inert on my cobwebbed ridge. Sighting myself in the same fleapit with cobwebs. I've been to school, and I'm hard wage earner, my mind travailed. But that wasn't the case. Tutelage without tenacity is like a plane devoid of an aviator.

I wasn't the only refined youth, as I wasn't the lone existing in a pit. Flipping my awareness through the contrivances of the prodigious icons of the eras that oscillated the world positively. The baffling was the state of the world. They've wrought, but the world is still in anonymity. Then I could see how the stars were shining in their enormousness, while the sky loitered in inconspicuousness.

Cruising my awareness through the names of the few phenomenal men and women who subsisted, the protuberant leaders, singers, inventors, etc. muddled my thoughts. A question emanated forth, and then I craved to ask my tutor. What I couldn't fancy was the baffling in my mind.

The unearthing was enormous. I could perceive that several prodigious men and women have lived and are still living, while the world loitered a ghetto. Many stars are shining perkier, but the sky dawdled dark. There's a space for every brilliant and imminent star. None should whinge of no prospect, for there's interstellar. Trying to authenticate myself if I wasn't insane, I dreaded.

Then, delineating the courtesy of my tutor, I asked him the question I plagiarized from my inquisitiveness. "Who're those in the ghettoes?" I delved. I actually craved to know, in other to comprehend my stance.

Amused, he said, "This is a very good question, because several have deliberated the ghetto as a quarry wherein lone the vetoed and unserviceable wits are living." He felicitated my methodology.

Galvanized by his jauntiness, I sat, primed to be spurred. I knew that he will tell me what I anticipated.

"There're commonalities in categories of those in the ghettoes, amid which are:

Hustlers!

This term denote to folks who extant out of woe and rigid life. They're the core sort of those you grasp in the ghetto. This genre of person's noshes out of perspires and skirmishes. Lots of them are acquainted to the tough life.

Some of them are not in acquiescence to any in authority. They cogitate that they're the monarchs to themselves. This category can be discourteous and reciprocal by exploiting anything that seems best to them, even if it mean assassinating, with motives flawless only to them, they won't care. They're taught and controlled by their cruel living panache. This sort may not be found in all ghettoes, but they're hard to be decimated from this dogma.

A hustler has this mentality, 'anything that can feed me as a bustle for today, I will do it, no matter what it may be,' because of this, they don't paragon any prerequisite to maneuver for tomorrow. They'll say,

'We never can tell the future.' Their lives are sentient all for today, 'What will I do to eat today?' this hustlers doesn't rely amply in the imminent, they rely on what they're seeing now to wad their belly. They will say, 'if you don't have or not alacritous in aiding me now, then I don't need you'. To them, counsels are like trying to make them snooze the more in their fate. They're taut towards conversion to an optimistic lifestyle, but tame if altered. They can be virtuous, if assimilated by an optimistic amendment." He ended.

I was heeding acutely and evacuating the Schneider pen-ink on carton smithereens in my dirty old rejected village plank cottage. Scrawling down everything he said, as a superlative scheme to custody the sagacious acumens.

"And the subsequent sorts of folks we find in the ghettoes are:

The Indolent!

They're the cantankerous type. They always lay it on those that uninhibited them, using the authorities as pretexts to their languor. This category has minutiae that have naught to do with their living in the ghetto. They are habitually as the strategic cogent to persons in the ghetto. They're the superlative edifice in charge of implementing their wobbly verdicts. They will not do anything that will augment a sanguine form of live of those in the ghetto. They've whys and wherefores in all the languorous acts they commit.

The Erudite!

We also have the intellectual in the ghetto, which requires prospects to divulge their astuteness, but no means. Their anticipations are condensed by those they regarded. After the family spending all on, he/she has zilch to do, at the end retreat to meet the parents in their ghetto stage. They believe that someday, something noble may occur that will mend their ghetto juncture of life. They're the optimistic type in the ghettoes, though riled and blur.

Note this, 'you must not stay in the ghetto to titivate it with your star. You can live out and do it,' be sentient and disposed. This type are educated and vivid, but in the ghetto.

The Valiant!

There're the plucky. Those who're acute to bulwark the veracity of others. They are not just living for themselves, but are concern about the affairs of others. They're spontaneous about those known as the 'forces of order'. They solitarily take upon themselves the bond to stand for others, even though procuring naught from them. They are alacritous and fitted to do anything for others defend.

The Battered!

There're the abused, in the ghettoes. This sort is deprived of their rights. They are living on the clemencies of felons. Their privileges are battered by those trying to hover, via the shoulders of others. Their moment of blubbering is their most comfy instants. Those are living with the imprints of agony within their hearts, shut-in with no one to expunge. They can be grasped, if avenged. They are with hopes that one day, their antagonists will be devastated. These are those who believe that, 'there's God,' who will assert them one day. They're bursting with optimisms on 'one day.' They are uncluttered to give in to any obliging alteration.

The Wicked!

Debauched folks are pervasive, including the ghettoes. There's no optimistic derivation in being wicked to any. That's why their tomfoolery is not exempted from, 'all impishness are not equitable.' Wickedness is a choice. By their own optimal, they've decided to be wicked, even to their fellow hustlers. They are not wicked because they are in the ghettoes, or because of the way they are been treated, but because they choose to be so…"

Then he told me the story of a man. It was so poignant…

He said. "A man once said, 'I don't kill because I want anything, but when I feel as to.' This is wickedness. There's nothing that can induce a wicked man to kerb or dawdle in wickedness than his choice."

Then he unremitted with the inspirational lessons…

The Virtuous!

"The good are also found in the ghettoes. Folks that have unambiguous to live their lives beneath the pedestals of unbiased dregs. They're unequivocal to loiter in buoyancy, in spite of the malevolent enclosed environs. These categories have made up their minds for the superlative. They've nurtured it as their ethos, to be noble in all statuesque. It's a choice to be good. It takes a tenacity to be upright in the hub of aches and felonies.

This type can aid in the ghetto towards others, for the good of those in the ghetto. They've decided not to be contingent, but to bid to those in the ghetto." My tutor terminated here, for I had to repose. It was late.

TWO

SITUATIONS AND SOLUTIONS IN A GHETTO

"Oh, the service was good today." I responded, to one of the passengers who knew me, while in the taxi. I was back from the prayer meeting in church. "Lots of singing, hullabaloo, crying, convoyed by prayers." I said, it sounded humorous as one of the commuters in the taxi spurt into hilarity. I wasn't flippant. That's the African Pentecostal way of venerating God. I was exhilarated of it though.

"There's no fix cypher in adulating God. Besides, God isn't man to pace with cryptograms; neither is he a respecter of man. Above all, he grasps the core and not the screeches of charlatans." Said one of the commuters beside me.

"Do you mean to say that there're phonies in basilicas today?" the taxi man probed. The umpire, at least. I'd snatched from his shrugs that he coveted to cope any miniature prospect to hurdle into the chat.

"You won't hear it from my mouth." The other passenger retorted.

I analyzed that he'd said that because I was around. Perhaps because I was a proselytizer, or to expurgate the story short. I will take it a type, was his considerations for sure.

"But I think folks yell because they're enthused by their glitches in the presence of God." Said a young lady, sited next to me. She'd actually avowed my thoughts.

"That's because those priests will bid them false optimisms that their hitches will go." The first passenger reacted. I was trotting off serenity, as my nerves tautened. Retorting will exacerbate matters, as I decided to clutch my antagonism.

"Africa is agonized in lots of things since time passed, as they're still travailing. And this's because we're in pursuit for easy life that cannot be assimilated just like that." The taxi man replied. Everybody giggled. None could really catch it briskly, as heads oscillated towards him. I couldn't contract it either.

That's why he'd unambiguous to drudgery with his taxi, I reasoned. Was that actually what he meant?

"I'm not in any church, because all those so call prophets, pastors, apostles…, are out for cash, so they use all tools to attain their target." The other passenger said. Laughter continued.

"I think I should halt this taxi drudgery and go and open my own church." The driver alleged.

He wasn't remote from veracity, for that's what is common in Africa. Several are still ready, as myriad are hazarding diurnally into the new lucrative trade. From here, ideas from my previous lessons started rustling to my cognizance. Not forgetting my hoary rejected village plank cottage, with an old dirty rejected double-seat couch as my bed, I had a question to ruminate on, during siesta. But that will be tomorrow, I reasoned. I was very tired. It was evening. It's been days that you haven't ruminated on your pristine world, I reasoned. I elongated myself on my habitual spot, divan. The involvement in the taxi – from my way back from the church – circumnavigated leisurely to my cognizance. Hearing the dawdling vernaculars, my realm was leisurely conveying me laterally. The question I had, collide my core, as I ruminated on those I routinely encounter when I go to eat in the indigenous restaurant at the hamlet square.

Why folks in the ghetto? My cognizance conveyed the query. Staring my dirty old cobwebbed roof, my back dashed amid the unembellished laths of my bed. Nosy to extricate why people will crave a stay in a ghetto, my awareness travailed. But, was assassinating ourselves out from this world going to healthier states? Maybe we will re-exist in a more enhanced way, I reasoned. Is it within our hegemony to take ourselves off from this ghetto, called life? Is it within my proficiency to take myself from this dirty old stinking rejected village plank cottage in which I anticipated diurnally for eras very far from impending? I mused rigid. Dared face-to-face to my grilling, life seemed bigoted to me. Cheers to my tutor, he eavesdropped me, and he was ready to riposte.

Loitering for minutes, he said, "There're perpetual whys-and-wherefores why persons are wherever they are, heedless to its formulation. Entities have altered aims why where they are. Some are there because of their peeved phase of life in the society. Others are because they can't thrive outside ghetto. I'll tell you several minutiae here ahead..." He assured me, as I concoct my intellects to snug the data.

Those with no Choice!

Those that have no choice outside ghetto. This type are sampled by frustration, to the extent that they have no further preference than to divulge the ghetto, as their abode. If they'd a choice, they would've preferred to inhabit among those whose life is sweet.

Here's what a star said: Quote… *If I'd the choice of proposing about myself and fate, I would've suggested to augment a bit in scope and worth in this dark cosmic sky.

None would ever choose to be a-no-body in this life of somebody. These ones, circumstances have impelled them to forcefully foster their fall in a forceful standard in the ghetto.

Those with a Choice!

These ones have picks on where they should fit. A man loped off royalty because he loved his ritual, and craved to live and die by it in it. So he went to the ghetto, where tradition was adept.

He'd a choice to make, and he made the choice of belonging in his ghetto. Not all are in the ghetto bereft of choice. There're folks who've preferred to be there, with delicate reasons. Don't be precipitous to clinch on those in the ghettoes. There's always tenacity, in everything that takes place in life. These are those, who are relishing their ghettoes in blubbing compunctions, while in hush.

A man unambiguous never to do something that will earn him a living, for he asserted never to call a parallel mortal as him, 'sir' or 'ma'am.' And because of that, he loitered in his ghetto phase of life in woe. There're many who've choices to make that could boost their ghetto stage of life, but because of specious picks, they linger in the ghetto.

A lady once said, 'I prefer to linger single, than to acquiesce under a man.' There're in misery for their erroneous assortments, which are habitually laid on nemeses.

Quote… Choice is the fuel to purpose…

Those Comfortable!

A skunk is comfy when in the mire. A goat is glowing while eating grass. A dupe is elated when in a garbage. There're people who're gratified in their ghettoes. One can be mollified where his/her prerequisites are met. There're folks whom their needs are quashed in the ghettoes.

A man unambiguous to convert into a scrounger, because he didn't hanker drudgery to earn a living. He thought it wise that his prerequisites will be met through beseeching. He went to the ghetto. There're people who are comfy in their ghettoes. This type, their alteration can come from the ghetto, since they wouldn't like to go out of their ghettoes.

There are supplementary motives. These few are to pageant that there's none in the ghetto devoid of a reason. If you don't know ones motive-of-being in the ghetto, you may not be proficient to aid. 'When there is a reason, there's a request.'" He terminated.

On the spot, the whim to aid Homo sapiens escalated from the nadirs of my unabridged. I could latch a carbon copy of myself as one of the elucidations of humanity, though an unfeasibility. Trying to focus on the pic, how can I verve about it? I hazarded. Educing his courtesy, I knew he was somnolent, bombshell. Could it be lassitude? He'd told me that I will comprehend him with time; I was leisurely clutching who he actually was. The foreboding was exigent, "How can one aid those in the ghettoes?" I probed. At least he's my tutor, it was his onus to instill in me what I anticipated.

Deliberate that it was my last question for the day. He retorted, "The trajectory in abetting those in the ghetto is a profound rifle. As ghettoes swerves from the alternative, so is the trail to aid those there. 'If you can succor one in the ghetto, then you can eliminate him from the ghetto.' Here're some views onward. The things you are to know are: …

Insinuate the Need!

What's the one you anticipate aiding necessity? If you can't insinuate a prerequisite, then you won't abet situations. The nature of the necessity will articulate if you can aid matters. Anyone in need knows what he wants in its nature. If you can't detect the need, then you can't cosine him.

A puckish lad, who'd loitered for days bereft of food, loomed to the priest, his pastor, as his last hope. Whinged of giddiness, saying that he has been for days without food. The vicar urged him to kowtow for litanies. After the prayers the youngster dawdled despondent, demise.

The vicar couldn't segregate the nature of the dude's need. He murdered the young acquitted puckish lad. He prayed on one that needed food, and not litanies. Prayers are good, but not in this case. What the person you're antedating to aid in the ghetto need is more vivacious, than what you have to bid. Know what the one in the ghetto need.

Be Able to Love!

Love the one to be abetted. There'll be no feat if one can't feel for the person to be aided in the ghetto stage. One must have a core that can sense for somebody, before he can succor the person. Those in the ghetto needs much love. Let what you do to those in the ghetto, have much to do with 'within' than, 'without.'

Quote…A heart cannot shelter, if it can't carry…

Those who love unequivocally are commonly folks with paucity to bid to the society. It takes love, to keep aiding the one who will never pageant gratitude for your exertions.

Go to the Ghetto!

A meager scrounger, who constantly seat at the road-side to solicit for cash from those transient. While fleeting, coins were layered in his pan, without a 'hello'. And there was this officer, who always passes through the road diurnally to his bureau. Upon his daily passage, he will bid a handshake to this skimpy scrounger, with a sincere 'good morning' through his lips. He would do that every morning, on his way to work, and in the evening, on his way back from work, without bequeathing a kobo to the dismal panhandler.

The officer did that until this day he was transmitted to work in another borough. He came to bid this meager scrounger cheerio handshake. On his way to the office to for his transferal permit, he offered the habitual handshake and said, "This is the last time I will be passing here. I am transferred to work in a different station". He said…

While he still talked, the poor beggar prattled into blubbing. The officer was flabbergasted, as he heard the meager scrounger said, "Amid all those I routinely meet on my circadian pedestals, you're the lone that usually rejuvenate my day". He said.

This officer delved himself. How is this plausible? Moreover, I've never given money to this man. What does he mean by this? He thought.

The scrounger said, "What usually fetch me at this kerb is not cash, but one who will bid me an erudition of belonging in the society, by at least chatting to me in this my ghetto stage of life. You're the lone who habitually do that, and not the coins and notes that folks will drop in my pan without a word".

This officer was the unique, who would brand this man's prospects contented diurnally. Those in the ghettoes need you more than the way they may be craving your chattels. Go close to them, and get to know them even better. Artless communication with one in his ghetto might do what your financial expectancy can't. One of the reasons why we have those in the ghettoes who are recalcitrant is because, they feel secluded, and vetoed by those adept to redeem them.

Sort out your Ghetto!

Comprehend that you're from a ghetto, before you'll be adept to aid another. Others cogitate that there're folks who're worse than some. One is worse in his constituent, and you, in yours. One cannot be impeccable in all. What you can give to one who has everything is hope for the one who has nothing. Therefore, all requires succor.

You need to know that there's naught like the last sort of humans. We all are in the global ghetto, whereas needs diverges in each minor ghetto.

Your school maybe well-structured and well-kept than mine, we're all students. Your ghetto maybe more archetypal than mine, but all ghettoes. If you don't know that you're from a ghetto, you will approach one in his erroneously." My tutor finished. The homilies where extensive. Taking a siesta and a piece of bread was the uttermost, to galvanize my forte…

THREE

THE SKY AND STARS

It's night, my cognizance yelled. Wow! The stars are out, heterogeneous and perky, I divulged. Elongating myself on my terrace for alternate encounter and curricula. My pen detained, as my jotter stationed on the stool obverse me at my porch, in the demises of the night.

I was furnished to jot down minutes, for I knew that the deliberation with each star wasn't going to plummet to the ground. Anxious to speak with the stars, my cognizance elated me from the dregs of the physical. Minutes later, I was conveyed to chat with the stars. I was augmented from my mind.

My preceding lessons about the ghetto grotesquely cruised through my cognizance. I could see how they are in reciprocal with the stars, having a lot in common. Then my tutor imparted in me the ensuing…

Approaching, he taught me the subsequent, "Your ghetto is your sphere of maneuver. The inevitabilities in each sphere swerves. Every ghetto has necessities. There're always major needs that want to revivify your star. It takes a full sentient being to grasp the major needs in a ghetto. You may not be mollified in life if not doing the veracious in a factual place, which is, 'shinning your star in your ghetto.'

No matter how remote you are, your ghetto is incessantly gaping for your star. It's chivalrous never to exist, than to occur and not marque a stimulus in your ghetto with your star, which I call, 'warped fate.' There're people who are innate in their ghettos, and others who're not, but everybody has a ghetto. To clutch your ghetto is one thing, and to luster your star is another. All needs may never be met except the prime ones. One's major necessities can still be another's trivial and vice versa." He ended, leaving me to the stars. I was indubitably exhilarated as I clasp him gabbed.

All stars are trifling!

Perpendicular in the core of the naught, my nadirs bogus forth this word, 'all stars are small,' it elicited the courtesy of my tutor to gyrate towards me, he was primed to divulge more to me. But how is this? I delved, perceiving bigger stars amid. Obviously, I needed ancillary elucidations analogous. Then my cubicles began enabling a philosophical understanding to my brain, as I caught the object for such an avowal.

He unremitted, "Heterogeneous are aggrieved from botch to segregate their ghettoes, and others because they haven't noticed the vivacity of their stars in theirs. There's none devoid of a ghetto. Your star maybe gargantuan to your acumens, the sky is vast but perpetually trivial to the eyes of the sky (ghetto) beholders. Those watching the dark sky always diminish stars because there's a discrepancy amid the aloofness from them and the sky (ghetto). No star grasps him trifling in assessment. Despite the horde of stars, he's still pugnacious to gloss, on tenterhooks to be seen in the eclectic sky (ghetto)." Mind-set, I understood.

While next to a star, he'd certainly been heeding my tutor chats. Revolving towards me, he static his stare. Hauling my unabridged courtesy in his itinerary, tautness rose from my unexpurgated, as I tweak forth a word of salutation.

Grinning, he moseyed handier. I grasped that he coveted to tell me something. What may that be? I speculated. Minutes later, he ruptured the hush. "Here we don't speak much." He said. Do stars talk? I could mooch as well.

Fostered at that, "What do you mean sir?" I probed, necessitating heeding the motive for such a word. Maybe they don't want to talk with me, I reasoned.

"Here we speak in enigmas that entail elucidations for comprehensive indulgent." He said.

I grinned, for he'd just the anticipated by me. I had heterogeneous questions, but few sheets for the answers. "That might be because of the elfin time we're been prearranged to vivify the dark sky. So we've to be fast, at least." He said.

"Is true sir, time is exquisite, and should be well fared." I replied.

"You sound nosy towards the gen of subterranean astuteness. I am only here to aid you, go ahead and probe any of the stars, and they'll reply you." He said. "I will be here to prompt you, when your time is bushed." He ended.

Then I perceived that he was but my chaperon. Revolving round, all the stars are busy in vivifying the dark sky, they were all serene. Adjacent to my lateral was one, looping handy, he was trivial but alluring in size. There wasn't any name to denote him, since they were all stars and copious. Lobbing to him my paramount probe, I vacillated for his antiphon.

"Greetings sir." I greeted. Amending my cognitive for the bubbly query. I knew that the dialogs were going to be a mesmerizing one through their gesticulations. Without qualms, "Sir how do you cope with your size in this horde?" I asked. Observing him acutely, he grinned rapt on his shinning. Feeling respite, I was certain that he will talk back. Finally! He said…

Quote… *we may be many in number, but the sky is still too big to contain only us…*

Wow! What a profound reason, my cognizance yelled. So deep, his reason was. I leered as my acuity inaugurated sketchily in this new world of the mind, as the star supervened with the ensuing…

Quote… *so long as there still remain dark vast places in the sky (ghetto), more stars are needed to fill the vacuum, that's why I exist…*

Then my tutor imparted me the ensuing through the lessons from these star, "Everybody would've been mollified if all had caught this exposé. Your ghetto needs you and your star.

Quote… *Despite the smallness of a star, there's no invisible star in the sky (ghetto)…*"

Lettering it in my petty jotter with copious ardor, I was ready as the impulse helix from my nadirs for auxiliary of the plangent adages. Time not affording me the fortuitous to ask him for itemization, I was glad to comfy it the way it emanated. Forfeiting copious courtesy, he unremitted.

Quote… *The size of a star does not frighten another of his future. To the stars, every day is today…*

Quote… *my size is not small for impact; I may not be qualified, but the sky (ghetto) is meant for me despite my frequency…*

Quote… *the smallness of my friend does not and will not discourage me. The more they are small, the more I'm seen among…*

Then my tutor continued from the words of the star. He said, "Are you seen amid? Despite the compactness of anonymity (state of those) in the sky (ghetto), there's no indolent star in the sky."

As I chatted with my tutor, a lesser star articulated to this other star in grins, as they both chuckled. Then I perceived that they were relishing their current stage. Here are the words he said…

Quote… *I am not intimidated by the way you shine, even though a star bigger than me appears in the sky tomorrow, after all, I've shine today…*

Quote... *If people smiles today looking at the sky because of my presence, I think tomorrow will be better if many of us are added, or better still some one bigger than me for the continuity of their smiles.

Quote… *If many come tomorrow, or one bigger than me, then I will remain an icon because I existed before them.

Then my tutor told me, "A star does not fear tomorrow. Rather, his quintessence is in today on vivifying the dark sky (ghetto)."

Quote… You're not too small for impact…

Quote… *My size to people may be small because they look at me from afar, but my brightness attracts human attentions and penetrates the tick darkened sky (ghetto). Therefore, no matter my size, I love my value in the sky and to the eyes of those watching.

Quote… *to make one still see the sky attractive despite the tick darkness, I have noticed that it is not by size or amount, but your worth to the sky through your star (for everyone is a star)…

Fascinated to heed smaller stars speak, I unambiguous to exchange only with trivial stars for that day. Galvanized by the acumen exhibited, I paced ahead to speak with other stars. Cruising contiguous to another smaller star in size, I asked, "Sir, how do you feel when you shine small?" He told me…

Quote... *Though I'm small in size, and my small presence is not permitted to shine for 24 hours round the clock, but I'm happy because I put in my best within the small period of time I'm permitted to brighten the sky in my small department…

Quote… *If I was not small in the sky, I don't think I would've been fortunate to shine in the sky of multitude of us and in this same sky of a one big light (sun) shinning at a time…

Quote… *My size is as an opportunity for me to be seen in these process of making the sky (ghetto) a hopeful better place, for those that needs smiles on their faces and there is no light to do that in their night times, that's why I'm a star…

From here, I went to the minutest of all the stars I encountered, and his reply was deep. Here're the words I acquired from him…

Quote... *If in the night someone can still smile looking the sky because of my presence, and their pressure taken away, then my size is not the problem…

Quote... *I am happy because I am not too small to make someone smile and his pains taken away. I'm happy to be a small star in this vast dark sky (ghetto)…

This was the last star I met for that day. Their time was up; they'd to pass the segment of the earth to a different route. After all, I was still a mortal; I had to repose for tomorrow. I vouchsafed to be there again tomorrow, same time.

Still at my veranda.

Moving into my dirty old village plank cottage, to relax on my filthy hoary vetoed sofa, and serene my hassle wits on the arm of the tattered divan, in other to condense the subterranean acumen from the stars for a forte tomorrow. "Good night!" I wished my neighbor, who sat at her portico, next to mine.

She'd been scrutinizing me punctiliously. I'd elapsed that the house-lord came for the five months' rent payment debt I owed. She'd strained encouraging me, not knowing that I relished my new found world. From her looks at me, she without qualms commiserated me. "Pastor good night." She replied. Standing, she went into her studio.

FOUR

THE RIGHT PERIOD FOR STARS

My countenance ice-covered, my mouth tautened and tasting syrupy. My assessment glowered, as I unbolted an eye. The sunlit flashed my eyes, as it coerce through the duds amid the staves of my village cottage. I'm on my couch, bed. Whacked on my dirty old rejected bed, with my head retained on its arm. I heard children rustling to school.

"Be fast, we're one hour late." A child said from outside, as they sped to school.

It's 8am! I reasoned. Classes start at 7am. There was still time for me to go and eat some corn-and-beans. 75france was in my worn-out stale murky primeval sandals. You were to go to the workshop today, my mind prompted me. I had to go to jostle for the day. I was in a ghetto, where I was determine in becoming a star.

At the workshop.

It's noon!

The sun is scorching, as I perspired. Struck with lassitude, I sat, looking up. There're no stars during the day, I thought. There, my sentience augmented, my wits tensioned as this question bash in my acumens. When is the actual retro for stars, and why? The question.

Sedentary on my old dirty rejected couch, I'm just back from the workshop. Taking a bath, there was some little cash from the day's drudgery, I ate. My hands draped on my chest, my legs folded on the brother-arm to which was my head.

Ruminating on this query rigidly. Minutes later, an answer cruised progressively to my lenient fetching more daintiness. Not mollified with the riposte, I had to interlude, to ask my tutor and the stars at night, since my teacher was bushed. The work had a lot to do with mental cunnings. Just few hours to dusk, siesta will foster it.

Up from my repose, my tutor was able to explicate on the matter, as my body stretched on my bed. He taught me the ensuing. "A man once delved the motive why stars do shine lone at nocturnal and not during the day. The question was and is still scrupulous…

The response to this question was: 'it's because there's no vacancy for them to shine during the day. The day doesn't need stars,' the better they keep shinning in the night, the best for them…

'A star that was elated each time they stare at him in the night during his dazzling moments was no longer fascinated in shining in the nocturnal, so he left and started shining during the day. After a while, he perceived that for some time now, no one has stared at him as usual. He was blurring till this day he asked someone this question:' 'why is it that when I shined at first during the night, you eulogized me as I luster. But now that I am shining during the day, no one clasps interest in beholding me as you usually do at first with your wife outside. What is happening'? And the star was stunned as he heard the man said: 'we don't need stars in the day because we can't see, feel, or even find their worth. The light is big enough to satisfy us'…

The star saw that he's derisory devoid of anonymity. He'd to return back to his ghetto and shine where he doesn't like. He unambiguous to go and gleam where he doesn't like because he coveted veneration once more. It's much about others in less you. When you look at the sky during the day you'll notice the existence of no star for they were not meant for the day. It's lone at night that one sees their visibility."

Quote… *The value of a star is vacuity without obscurity, the splendor is devious devoid of a dark sky (ghetto), her grin is deeming without an unlit background.*

Gratified by the astute paradigm acumens, my cognizance travailed as I paranoid some qualms. Waiting for the stars in the evening, my face zigzagged habitually out-and-in, queuing their occurrence.

It's 8pm and there's no star yet? My awareness probed. Waiting copiously was the lone cypher to meet them in a virtuous state. At my veranda, my system remorseless the waiting. Not sapped by the 4hours queuing, I hassle-free my back on the plank wall.

Minutes further, my serenity was increasingly waning away, as I speculated if stars were going to come out. Ambiguous by one of my ghetto area boys that came around, for a visit. Chatting with him for about 30minutes, he left. Returning to my veranda, there were stars. Oh, thank God! I articulated gratitude. I couldn't wait to be elated by their presence.

This time around, I was primed to allot much time with him. Impending the first star, I probed, "Sir, how do you sense ensuing in the dark?" I couldn't deferral. Perceiving that he was elated to have me ask a question, his fervor pacified my whole. Then he said…

Quotes… *I can thrive in the dark, which makes it a phenomenon to sundry. I'm a subject to the world because am a subjugator in the dusky…*

I used this question as a ruse. Not mollified by his riposte, the need for this query ensued in me, as I asked. "Why do you choose to gleam but in the dark?" Today was predominantly for questions. It could be deliberated puerile by him, but I was hazed on what will cradle a star to shine in the night, when those that were hypothetical to appreciate them are bushed, and others asleep.

I wouldn't love to shine where none will appreciate me. Not the night. Then I was startled by the answer he gave. I tacit that the prime drive isn't doles. Then what? Here's what he said…

Quotes… *It's not easy to repel the dark and secluded jiffies and still divulge virtuous optimistic reflexions in your elfin size…*

Quotes… *It takes an intrepid, gritty and audacious man to do that. I'm happy because I am gritty and audacious enough to repel the impulse darkness and still divulge my magnificence...*

Quotes... *You like you nap and contravene my presence during the dark moments that happens to be the only time I have to be seen, I'm happy because I am having fun as a star...*

Quotes... *Don't do it because you want ovation from people...*

Quotes... *A star doesn't shine with the aim to be praised, but because he needs a sense of belonging.*

While chatting with the other star, one of the stars close to me, who was surely eavesdropping us, exclaimed in a loud tune...

*Quote... *If I don't shine in the dark, I won't be seen in the day...*

Quote... If you don't shine in your dark world, you won't be seen in the lighted world...

*Quote... *than to fear the dark and die in the dark of inexistence, better to overcome the dark and be seen in the existing darkness...*

Subsequently, the ideas of all that I saw on my roof, while on my dirty old rejected couch of a bed the other day collide my wits profoundly, as thoughts about my ghetto emanated to my view. Then my teacher imparted me something that instigated me to ascertain some prodigious stuffs. Here was the lessons from my tutor…

Staring at me acutely, he said, "I have seen that it is good to be in your ghetto and be seen than to be out of your ghetto and be obscure. All stars would wish to shine in the day to embellish the day, but because it is not good to befuddle those working in the day by their splendor, they're obligated to shine in the dark (ghetto). Stars shines in the night." He deciphered my query…

After the chats, a germane question escalated in my core. I was distraught by it to the extern I couldn't clutch it any more. Divulging it forth was the lone way through. "What's your role model?" I asked. I was beginning to sound indiscreet, I knew, but not to worry. From life, I'd erudite that there's no design without a template.

None articulated a word. Then my tutor spoke forth, I felt euphoric heeding him talk. Here was what he tabled to me…

"The stars and sun have an analogous assignment but not the same knack, that's why the sun is the role model to the stars." He said.

As I thought, the star spoke out. The answer was unerringly what I anticipated. But afraid to counter it down orally, for not to humans was I denoting, my neighbors would ruminate me as a mental deranged. I was alone in the dregs of the corporeal. I could eavesdrop this new world of opinions audibly, athwart to the streets from Bakingili to Douala.

Heeding my tutor is fluent in, one of the stars said avariciously …

Quote… *my role model is the sun because the sun is a success…

Then I could spontaneously prompt my assessments apropos life as the phantasmagorias of the altered units of life were cruising to my survey. Then my tutor said in glee, "I have noticed that anything you take as a role model, you stand behind."

Quote… You are under anything you take above you in life…

From his words I was in a bombshell as muddle collide my cognizance ensuing the avowal of this other star. It was profound, as I craved for auxiliary elucidations on the topics. Staring at them acutely without a word, one star said…

Quote… *Because of the sun I am what I'm daily. My victory in the dark depends on the success of the day. The sun is my role model because I aspire to be like him in the future…

My cognizance divulged her own findings. Understanding impending ubiquitously as my cranium stationed. Not intuiting the ach my neck unbridled. Besides, I was out of the canal. I was also nebulous in the corporeal world of carnalities, narcissisms, and friction, to where everything is innate – the mind. I was jammy.

Minutes later, my tutor said, "The stars would never love to be overcome by the dark one day, and the light has the conundrums to that. That's why the stars choose the sun as their role model. Collaborate in your ghetto."

Noticing that they're forfeiting courtesy and retorting my queries, I called forth a certain group of stars, and probed the same. "Why do you choose the sun as your role model?" The question.

Calling various stars will aid me get altered assessments to why the choice. I'd tacit that people have heterogeneous whys and wherefores they do what they do. I grew to swot that things don't just ensue. There's a reason why everything supervenes. Here was the response of the various stars…

*Quote… *I refuse to degrade myself, that's why I'm a star…*

*Quote… *I worked hard to sun my role model in other to become a star and I thought it wise to make the remain a star…*

My tutor intervallic by saying, "Hard work sorts a man, but noble verdicts retains him. Work hard and beyond all, think well. It's because the stars don't like to compete with the sun, that's why the stars chose to succumb to the sun."

And the stars continued…

*Quote… *I made the light my role model because I want a harmonious running of the universe…*

*Quote… *Nobody forced me into emulating the sun in any way. I noticed that only a star in a different department can make stars in other departments…*

Then my tutor said, "If the sun bid vitality to the stars, then the sun is above the stars. One cannot make another into becoming a star to rule together in the same constituency. It's informal for one to make another a star to rule in a different department. Many love to have associates and not contestants. Focus in your department." Profound, his words sounded.

The stars continued…

*Quote… *I made the light my role model because life is useless and establish-less without a teacher…*

*Quote... *after all we are governing but two different spheres. I made the sun my role model because two kings cannot rule on the same throne...*

*Quote... *I made the sun my role model because everyone needs a stencil in other to come out with the design of his/her life. Your design may not be as the same as mine...*

My cognitive clutched the ensuing, 'Give to the one superior to you the right honor, and you'll be honored in your state.' I am blessed at the profound acumens.

FIVE

WHY STARS IN THE DARK

"I'm tired", my tutor exclaimed, as I sat at my veranda. My mind was certainly bushed. Managing myself into my kerbed cottage, I napped on the old dirty rejected tattered double seat couch of a bed. "Father protects me." I said in shambles, beneath the dregs of fatigue. I was instantaneously conveyed by the spirits to the manors of temporal recreation. There, the spirits of the mortal are laid for impetus refreshment.

Chatters from the backyard impelled sounds of birds to wake me. It's morning, my sub-consciousness told me. I upstretched my cranium from the arm of my bed. That's Africa; birds are part of our gen philanthropists. Uncurling myself up, I raised for my morning onuses. I am exhilarated and jammy to stay in a village bush plank house, with its bare unpaved floor. Valeting the floor every morning, as it is the duty of most, wasn't my problem.

Siesta!

Let me ornate on my prior lessons of last night, I reasoned. Trying to focus on the last lessons; my interactions with the stars and my tutor. Profound, it seemed. Flipping through the various interactions, a question rose from within, as I began speculating about my previous teachings.

Why stars in the dark? My consistencies enunciated, aloud. My tutor paced in to aid me through, by elucidation. Then he said, "Instead of reigning and aiding the sun in revamping the day on their daily bases, why have stars unambiguous to fit and sequester themselves in the murky sky (ghetto) during the uninhibited hours of the nature? O stars, is it your choice or that of the nature? ...

I was muddled as he abetted in broadening the question. This wasn't an answer, for Christ sake. I needed an answer here, and not one who will succor in tallying salt in the wound. Understanding my idiosyncrasy, he continued.

…I will tell you all that you need to know about your question in the evening." He told me.

Was that all he was going to say? That wasn't still the answer I anticipated. I'll be with the stars in the evening. I hope he hasn't elapsed about that. Maybe he was going to tell me after my encounter with the stars. Serenity being the lone trail here, I had to take it, as I moseyed through to the evening.

Ready to speak with the stars, I sat outside. Waiting for them, as they cruised forth in their array. Bejeweled With exuberance, I stood beside one, and asked, "Why do you shine in the dark?" The question.

It wasn't outlandish to find out that one like me will anticipate stars to shine during the day, the nature of humans. Seeing the incentives of most parallel, I couldn't ruminate otherwise.

Few minutes later, he chortled, indicating disclosures, and said…

*Quote… *I shine in the dark because the day will not appreciate my efforts and value…*

*Quote… *I think it's good to shine where you will be seen, that's why I'm a star…*

From these two answers, I could twig the reason why people mostly outshine only where they're eulogized…

Quote… If you can't sense the accolades while in the field, then your worth may not be seen.

…I also noticed that the stars have used the dark sky as a prospect to showcase. I could as well note that there's an opportunity for everybody to be prodigious in life because of the state of the world. If only you can see it as an advantage, manage it well, and you will shine.

Then my tutor spoke forth, responding the major query in my intellect. In fact, it was the question that elicited me into this rifle of profound schemes of life.

These were what he said…

"You can flourish in life and change your dirty ghetto, by becoming somebody prodigious." He said.

Then I inaugurated chromatic aims why I shouldn't nosedive in life. Obviously, I needed a discrepancy from the double seat old dirty rejected couch of a bed, on which by body was arduous amid its unembellished hoary dirty laths. I wasn't born to dally in a dirty old tattered village plank cottage, though I might have been born inside. I knew that I couldn't do that without first fetching an alteration in me, it was under process.

My acumens detonated as I began seeing life as artless as I couldn't ruminate. Money was gradually circumnavigating into a servant to me, the lone boss who've marinated me austerely form birth. The reason for my meager stage was gradually becoming an advantage for me to challenge myself and drudgery with focus. Life was gradually becoming a gratifying duel, as I could see myself running through, having others elated as my prime goal.

My mind traipsed back to the game of football. I could see how I cavorted to latch the courtesy of aficionadas, it orbited about them. I was frolicking supplementary than I could, notching goals, and hailed at.

Life was gradually syrupy even as I had naught to exhibit for. The fable of, 'one came with naught, and shall return with nothing,' was copiously inferred to me. I began seeing more reasons why I should exert on how to make the world idyllic, and not laying diurnally on my dirty smelling old frayed couch, staring at the nauseating cobwebbed roof, waiting for a day that has never come since in my lineages waiting days, which wasn't ready to start impending. Being livid with the government, and those who wasn't there on the day of my formation. That was the utmost rash thing that stultified my tutor's voice from echoing in me from birth.

"You just discovered purpose." My tutor said.

I had to get back to what was before me. I had to heed more from their yawning maxims. Elated and reinvigorated on how to stratagem myself on how to augment the ghetto and not censure the way I see things. Then I equivocate never to scorn without a scheme. "No one has any reason to censure without a way forth. Better stay inaudible in that ache if you don't have a suggestion on a way out." My tutor said. He'd surely been construing my sulks.

Quote… Stars shine in the dark because nobody will appreciate their worth in the day. Your star can only shine where people can see and acknowledge your worth…

This other star, after scrutinizing our dialogs for a while, paced handier and asked a startling question. I wasn't good at responding questions. Brooding on the question, I illustrious that it was to be kept within myself. I wasn't there to teach them, or altercate what I knew with theirs.

*Quote... *if the dark sky (ghetto) will announce me, then why should I not be in it for my announcement?*

The question was profound, as I mused on. From this, I saw that there's no need to whinge, but darn your ghetto in any constituent you find yourself. Do your superlative. The star was indeed candid to him. He knew that if he shines during the day, he will not be of use to those in the world.

Then I grinned because it was parallel to me. I noticed that if I was in a luxurious house, having everything comprising a soft-family-size-bed with superlative china made settee, I wouldn't be sedentary outside at this profane hours of the nature. There were sundry aims to thank the nature for my current stage, though calamitous with it.

Should I thank God for what I don't like? Is it probable? Then my tutor ostentatiously articulated the story of a youngster, who receives bread from the father spotting biscuit on his other hand, which happens to be what she craved. She thanked the father with the notion of pleasing his heart to gain the biscuit, than to whine and stop him from procuring it the next time.

Musing on the inane story, I hummed unobtrusively. Beholding another contiguous star, he spoke, as I heeded.

And here was what he said…

*Quote… *I am not in the dark only because I want to be announced, but because I will be announced without any conditions, stress, and depression…*

Here he divulged the motives of his shinning in the dark. There my cognizance drove back to my old dirty roof. I saw how I could use my stale chaotic room as a prospect for my shinning in this ghetto called life.

Heeding him amply, he unremitted…

*Quote… *I thought it necessary to shine in the ghetto, because it's my duty to do so. If I don't do it, none will…*

He was meant to shine in the dark. There's no flawless fate consignment devoid of a palpable lesson plagiarize from life. The day doesn't escalate his knack; therefore, he was destined for the night. After all, time is squat and should be treasured.

I was exhausted and necessitating some repose for forte tomorrow. Oh! It's 2am, my cognizance yelled. Spotting at my small Nokia cell phone. I was really tired. Elongating me on my dirty old rejected smelling couch of a bed. I slept.

The next day!

Converging on the astonishing lessons I erudite yesterday, I hankered for the night to fissure. The impulse to quiz them arose in me. My countenance nerd with elation, as one after an encounter with the cherished he so loves and craves to squash. My cognizance equipped, like that of a teen on her first date, face to the guy of her hallucinations. Euphoria soared in me like in a young man in his first 'yes' from the lady of his heart for the first experience.

Enthused from the esoteric, my pen snug in my hand as my block note sat before me, ready to be filled by the ink of the Schneider blue pen. On my terrace, I sat. It's 11pm, and all the stars were all out. I could see them everywhere in the sky, even the habitual deem ones were clear to my view.

Steady, I scrutinized the sky acutely. The questions of yesterday collide my wits for the second time, but lax and flawless this time around. "Why stars in the dark?" I asked, as I paced handier to the first star. He was vigorous and exhilarated to emanate contiguous for the answer. I fixated to heed his profound aphorisms. Ready to inscribe it down,

He said…

*Quote… *if I was meant to shine during the day, then God would've made me a little bit bigger than the sun…*

"Because stars where fated for the dark, it's noble to be where you belong, and not where you like or want to be." My tutor nippily prompted me.

Ruminating on this, a tinny star, I think he was the infinitesimal of all the stars in the sky, spun towards me and said…

*Quotes... *I shine in the night because apart from the dark, there is no other vast available sphere for me to be seen in this my little shape...*

After when he'd said it, my tutor told me this as a notice from the quote…

"There's a sphere in which God has made stars to shine, without which they may not be able to divulge their propensities." He said.

Then the first star unremitted, as I grasped that none can become a star without a dark sky, ghetto. Each person's ghetto is his sphere of maneuver, I noted. That's where one's occurrence and knack is needed. Where you'll gismo your flair devoid of acute for interest.

Quote... Praises don't come from expectations, but from perfections...

Quote... Life is not a giver but a gift; use the gift to give...

"Your presence and gift is the required for the furtherance of your ghetto." My tutor said,

The star continued…

*Quote... *I am in the ghetto (dark sky) because we – stars – have no value and worth without the ghetto (dark sky)...*

From here, I noticed that one of the reasons why people aren't gratified in life is because most of them are segregated from their ghettoes. Lone your ghetto can venerate you into the star you've always craved of becoming.

Quote... See that office, job, career, trade, country, etc. you crave, as a ghetto that needs your star for your shinning...

Heeding amply, I heard the stars bid their aims why they're superb in the dark and not the day. Then I ended with this other stars for today, as they said...

*Quote... *I shine in the dark because it is my duty to brighten the night though small in size...*

*Quote... *my size does not matter; I can still brighten the dark and lives...*

*Quote... *if it is me who will bring light, though not a great light in this my small size to the dark, then I must be honored...*

Then reasons were flawless as I unambiguous to ruminate like them, and above all, act like them. Because I will love to be a star someday. My assessments on other things were unsullied. Then my tutor spoke again.

Here's what he said...

"If you've the opportunity in your country, community, company etc. to fetch positive change, then you're privileged. Don't dissipate the chance, shine your star. 'I'm privilege to have this inaugural that can etch my name in the history of mankind.' Guise at it like that, and not on temporality." He halted.

Before I leave, I'd to ask this last question that effervesced in my cognizance. "What bequeathed you these knacks to convey such alteration in the dark?" I needed to know, because I would love to allot amendment in the world as well.

Here were their ripostes…

Quote… *I've brought change in the dark (ghetto) because I'm a change, not in my size, but in my quality…

*Quote… *I made myself valuable to visualize others in which the dark (ghetto) is a living testimony…*

Here I had to consent for another day. I needed to repose for I was bushed. Pacing inside, I slept. Comfy, my dirty old rejected smelling double seat couch wasn't any longer a nervous abode, but an atmosphere of forecasting a healthier tomorrow. Elated was I, because soon I wasn't going to be squatting in such a pigsty. Beholding my roof, there was obscurity; I could no longer see the torpors. I cruised in shambles, on the arms of the naught. Beneath the dregs of slumber.

SIX

DISCOVERING THEIR NEEDS IN THE GHETTO

It's another day,

Sedentary on the veranda of this my old dirty rejected village plank cottage, ready to obtain my life altering lessons. Leeches flipping ubiquitously. The cold is intense today. Dins from the music at the road-side are all-pervading my auricles, since my tattered village cottage wasn't far from the road. The bars are open, as the drunkard's yells are heard. From my veranda, I was ready to learn.

My cognizance unbolted, as my earholes became dismal from the corporeal.

Jiffies passed. Scrutinizing the sky acutely, as a thriving query raid my sanities. 'What's a star?' my awareness probed. Ostensible blur, at the same time striving towards the nature. Thoughts inaugurated cruising athwart my cognizance, as theories emanated handier to my grasp. Selecting which to clutch, a doppelgänger of a star appeared. Small as it was, I mused, as the answer floated to my sentience. Ready to heed,

My tutor taught…

"A star is that sole potential in an individual, which is in admiration of site, in other to be seen. Each person has a star. Anyone that has these lone potential is a star…

Quote… Carrying a star in you makes you automatically a star…

…The site that entails the conspicuousness of your star is your ghetto. Thus, if we'll have stars in us, then we all have ghettoes that necessitate those stars in other to be seen. Not all may have the same capacity of potential, but there's none devoid of a knack. We all have diverse flairs, as we have altered ghettoes that our stars are in veneration of." He said.

I've just learned about what a star is, and the atmosphere for stars. Knowing that there's none deprived of a star, I've just realized that I have one. Still profound in these thoughts of mine, another question emanated onwards, 'Which type of stars are needed in the ghetto?' My cognizance probed my tutor.

I needed to extricate the sort of stars that are needed in the ghetto, to know if I was amid. Muddy if a ghetto can have more than one star, I was decoyed as I asked about the stars required in a ghetto.

Then my tutor said…

"Heterogeneous stars are crucial in a ghetto, in veneration of their variances in utilities. A ghetto can have more than one star. Sundry stars can feat in shining in the same ghetto. Above all, never assert your stay and utility in a ghetto that doesn't need your star." He said, I tacit.

My eyes were flawless. Perpendicular contiguously to a star, I was in a bombshell at their audience to me. I felt like one of them. God forbid, I'm not in the dark, my cognizance fouled. The world isn't better from a dark sky. I couldn't alter the facts, though my scheme unremitted the deliberation.

Vertical, a star paced handier and dabbed my face, lo and behold, the shroud encumbering my sight fell off. I inaugurated seeing the stars as human beings, functioning in varied precincts of life. Flabbergasted at that, I shuddered. "Don't be fossilized. We would love that you should learn more." One of the stars said, putting on a blue jean trouser, and a grey jacket on a white T-shirt. I stared at him acutely, horrified.

Revolving round, ample folks were there, drudging. They were skivvying in manufacturing the sky a buoyant enhanced place in her night times. Probing for air, I clutched some, as I emanated unruffled in my nadirs. Ready to talk, a question coined to my cognizance. Seeing the stars at onus, in altered works of life. The sky was actually busy. Pinpointing one of the stars, "hello sir, can you please tell me about yourself as a musician?" I asked, seeing him singing.

He was a star artiste, standing with the microphone, giving a slow zouk – a kind of music found around the East Africa – that could crush the mandibles of every encumbrance and inaugurate buoyancies on the face of anyone under woe. Perceiving other musicians frolicking the various apparatuses, I waited for an answer.

Then he said…

*Quote… *I'm shining as a star in my musical ghetto-domain, and in it I need others who will shine in the instrumental domain as a star as well, and so on… that's why many of us are needed in this same ghetto…*

Galvanized by that, I needed to be fast. Pacing to the highway for a chat with the contractor, handling his contract meritoriously. Spotting everybody, busy, I paced handier to the contractor. I needed to situate myself busy for none was malingering there. "Sir, please can you tell me a little about yourself?" I asked the chief contractor in charge. I vacillated for an answer,

He said…

Quote… *I'm shining as a star in this road edifice trade in this country ghetto of mine as a star, and in it, I will need technicians who will shine along with me as stars in this same ghetto…

Heeding that, I wrote it down as I paced to one trifling farm contiguous. Seeing how busy they were, I had to ask, because I thought one could only shine in an office. Astounded at that, I had to ask to know about them.

Quote… *I'm shining in this farm ghetto of mine as a star, in it I will need those who will shine with me in making the hoes, machetes, etc. …

Amassing all of this, my tutor took the floor, as he aided me with the elucidations. This was all that he scrutinized from the happenstance…

"You become a star by unleashing your proficiencies in what you do in your ghetto. What you do, will make you a star, if you do it well. Stars are innate in the inside, and are become from the outside. What you do, and how you do it, makes you a star." He said.

As I look at all the people, they were so busy. There was this thing I noted. The farmers were not working on the road. The contractor was not managing the farming system. The same thing goes to the musician, and the rest…

There was a location wherein they wrought. Then my tutor told me, "Stars thrive because they're in veneration of site." He said. Knowingly well that stars only appears at night in the sky (Ghetto), then my whole fetched this as an inference to the location of stars for stars.

My tutor said…

"All stars are in reverence of scenery (ghetto)…

…Trees aren't grown in the desert. The sun is not made for the night, but for the day. Stars are not fated for the day, but for the night. The blanket is not for cold, but for warmth. There's a site for your star, which is the ghetto…

…Fate isn't ubiquitously, but somewhere. A fisherman cannot work, without water. Man may not dwell outside oxygen. Food is meant for the stomach, and the belly for nourishment. The fish cannot live outside the water. Your knack is naught, if not where it's required, the setting is vital…

…There's a place, where you're cherished with what you carry. You can have a prodigious flair to sing or act, and you get into the biggest musical and film industry, and not be heard because of incorrect motives. Don't be in a place with your star because you want people to help your star, but because you want them to be aided through your star, and you will shine." He said, flaring the eyes of my considerate.

All of this my tutor presented to me, conveying some specimens, as I learned and noted. Then I deliberated in my whole, why one with such skills to cultivate, sing, and construct, etc. wouldn't love to resolve in his homeland – Country – to revamp it into his star making, but would go for greener pastures in a land where none have ever found. What a Potty petty.

At the same peak, I conjectured on why one will be stuffed with all of this genii, and instead to move to the prodigious countries like USA, England, China, etc. for his star to inflate, he resolves to squirm on this obscure besmirched filthy hoary vetoed and smelling double-phase government, with their vertebrae beleaguered amid the sullied organization of pilfers, political fibbers, emotionless assassins, muted government, occultists, and a bribery-system country of no advancement in the tattered nasty embryonic and egocentricity continent in which we all live as in a nadir of no trail out. With our craniums tackled to callous emotionless wicked and mendacious governmental bunkums, which're shrouded with kismet, inanity, impishness, narcissism, and larceny diplomacies. Placed on the destitute armrest of brutality. What a potty petty.

Then one star contiguous, construing my cognizance, he said…

*Quote… *I'm shining in the dark, because I wanted those in the dark to be helped through my little light, in my little size, that's why I'm a star. Motives…*

Then my tutor said gaudily, "You may not triumph in a specious site. Locate your setting (ghetto), for that is where your star is really needed. Let your objects be flawless, be there because they need you, and not because you need them."

Disconcerted by the lessons I've learned. My cognizance was hefty and chubby, as I inaugurated trepidation that it could ignite. I'm just 21years, I supposed. Not able to fancy that I was the one procuring such cavernous stuffs. Ready to confront life, my cognizance divulged to me what I just perceived, "You've just learnt the criterion which is the tenacity for life." He said. Then my tutor inaugurated the summary of my phenomenal unearthing, so far.

He taught…

"If you can't ascertain a necessity in your ghetto, you may not be adept to fit in for sway. Your works will be entrenched lone on the plinths of what you have discovered. If there's a prospect in your ghetto, and stars are needed, which unit will you fit in for impact? Or will you just go because you are looking for probabilities to be seen? If you can't ascertain the prerequisite in your ghetto, you won't be proficient to outrival as a star. It's the nature of the need that will exhibit if you're needed there, of not…

…there're several means by which one can distinguish his ghetto. It is from the need, that you can know your frequency there. A singer may only outrival where music is needed, and not where you can sing or dance well. You may only outstrip where what you have is crucial, and not where you are impeccable in what you do…

Illustration:

…Despite the way late Michael Jackson sang and hove troops, there're folks who doesn't still like his music. And no matter the way you stab meandering your voice to be like him, you can never be him, and that divulges that you'll never pull the crowd he pulled, because your plagiarism will never be analogous…

…Distillate on your ghetto of utility, and halt trying to be another, for you will never be. Duplicate none and you won't be pugnacious behind any. In any arena you find yourself, don't be anyone else just be you. When you try to facsimile, you will always be trying to catch-up. Your ghetto needs you, and naught like the replicate of anyone else…

…We need to know that the world is an inclusive ghetto that comprises heaps of trifling ghettoes, in which discrete stars are needed for the furtherance of the world. Just know what your ghetto needs, for that is the foundation to your star…

Quote… If you can't realize the need, then you won't be realized in the need…

…What is the need for you volunteering into that trade? Is vital, and not how much you've kept for it? When you know the need, you can vaunt of your stance in what you anticipate doing in your ghetto." He told me. Then my whole conversed to me the more as I left for the next day. I was drowsy, pacing inside; I lay on my old rejected dirty smelling double seat couch. I slept.

SEVEN

THE NEED FOR STARS

– FESTIVITY –

The next day!

Dins ubiquitously. People fleeting in alacrity to the beach behind the house, to have their bath. What's happening? I conjectured. Necessitating someone to aid me out, for it's not habitually like this. Pacing out from my local cottage, "What's the matter?" I asked one of my neighbors, as she arranged her toddlers in the optimum of their garbs.

"Today is FESTAC in Limbe." She replied.

Wow FESTAC!

FESTAC is a one week annual Festival of Arts and Culture, celebrated in Limbe metropolis, once every year. It's an event that regroups all the villages that constitutes the Bakwerians, and other ethnic groups around the country.

Hastening inside, I got myself ready. I'd unequivocally elapsed about the announcement some days back from the town-crier. Maybe because I was conceded away by my new world. I love such fiestas, the FESTAC makes me reminisce the NGOUN Festival in the west region, fêted by the Bamouns. But that constantly takes place once in two years, towards the end of the year.

Though it was my first time attending FESTAC, but I knew that I was going to experience copious prodigious stuffs from what I've grasped in the NGOUN Fiesta. Cameroon being a Country of sister cultural heritage, they'd everything in mutual.

I love such revelries for her neutralities in everything such as the dances, racing, singing, cooking, and other cultural rehearsal that has a lot to do with our ethnicities and customs. Limbe FESTAC is one of the countrywide sporadic festivals that aids in revealing Africa's splendor in ethos. I couldn't afford to miscue the event; it was the seventh day, the last day of the show. Everything was going to be exhibited. The presence of the nationwide popular stars where there, what none would afford to miss.

An hour later!

I was on my way, in the taxi.

"Hmmm! My brother, today go hot." One of the guys with me in the taxi spoke out in the Pidgin English. Connotation that today is going to be splendid.

I was just next to him. The taxi was chockfull, as seven of us were in a five places taxi.

The atmosphere was bursting with exhilaration and prodigious prospects, as all could feel.

Traffic on the highway. Dances, as folks paced to the ceremonial ground a kilometer away. Sited inaudibly in the taxi, I observed the hygienic beach, and the neat environs, well bedecked. I love the city for its salubrious beaches, and pleasant edifice. Being my prime time attending it, I had a very little to chat about the event. My system torrid, my hints tensioned, as the anticipations were intense. I couldn't wait to experience. My eyes were elated on the things I beheld, and the magnificence of the things I've always heard since time past.

The place was well festooned in the metropolitan alongside the great Atlantic Ocean, the contiguous to the mount Cameroon. The altered local chiefs were seated. The government high personalities were chaired in, as the revelries soared in allure. It's indeed fascinating, my cognizance stated, as I saw the daintiness of nature curtailed for everyone's considerate.

I love this, my cognizance yelled. Unearthing folks ubiquitously as the tautness proliferated tick in the air. Minutes later, my awareness ensued off the show from the corporeal. I could see how the place was spontaneously altered. I saw flairs, denoting them as the stars. I grinned in inference that my time wasn't futile in my new world of thoughts. I was learning a chunk of what is existing.

Copious stars I saw that could be concerted on for the alteration of our ghettoes. The actual assessment of the world was substantially bare to me, as I gauged altered prodigious enactments. I called it 'the magic of mother nature given to us.' Its enigmas were underneath our rheostat. Some would call it talents, but I was seeing the nature illuminating the paradoxes of his magic to us. A profound sagacity of belonging collide me, hard, as I saw altered amalgamated retrospectives. Then my tutor hastened in, and taught me the ensuing…

The Need of a Star!

"We're living in a world of glooming obscurity sinister ubiquitously, making the necessity of your star more exigent to the endeavors. From the look at things, if our stars are not invested in this murky world, we won't be able to aid. If we can't see the needs of our personal potentials in our various ghettoes that makes the global ghetto, then we're in an error…

…The world would've been an enhanced habitation and not a toilsome precinct, if this was grasped some eras ago. Well, it's never too late to do well, we can still pick up with veracities. What can you do? Where can you do what you can? …

See the Need!

…If you can't see the need of what you carry, none will do it for you. You need to be venerated through yourself to others. Let not folks see you to your corollary, be the one to see yourself to your extrapolation. If you cannot see yourself, then none will see your actual self. If you can't hear yourself sing, none will heed you sing. If you can't see yourself ensuing, then none will see you a success.

It's a certainty that emanates from within, which is equipped to contravene challenges tackled on the way. Start seeing your real self. You have a star that just needs the sum of your courtesy to be exhibited. None will see your star, if you can't see it yourself…

Let it make a Way for You.

…Let your star make a way for you, you can't aid your star. What do you want to become? What can you do? Start with what you can, and strive to what you want, through your ability. There's always a way up in life. Look for the lane up. Inaugurate from where you are, and not from where you want. If you trail life the way it is, you will one day encounter the superlative. Ubiquitously perchance a way, rifle the way…

Trail Your Star.

…follow your star. Your star will allure all that you've perpetually craved. Ensuing your star is following the lot. Anyone who tracks affluence culminates the domestic to dough. Therefore, warrant your star, and coinage will aid you and your necessities. Let rejuvenating the sky, be your top-most precedence." He ended. Profound, the lessons where.

Back to my cottage!

The day was bursting with lessons. I'm about to face the first star for auxiliary chats. About dialogue in route with the event of the day at the FESTAC boulevard. I really craved to homily about the endeavors in our societies. This opinions has been with me through from the ceremonial ground to my cottage.

Perpendicular adjacent to the first star. A question about to nerd through my orifices, I tardy for the last jiffy to speech it forth. "What's your primacy as a star?" I asked.

I ached to know the resolve of his gritty shining knack in the dark. I've once deliberated on this with them, but I wanted to understand it much better. I was alacritous to luster as a star in the world as well, if the prospect is given me.

Then he said…

*Quote… *my priority is to brighten the sky, and beautify it in the dark, and not to be praised by any. That's why I was there before any of you came into existence…*

Blur as I heed this, ache bashed my core, as I mused auxiliary, in line with what he just said. My shining anticipation was motived on the accolades behind, at least for an alteration from my murky vetoed hoary reeking double seat bare settee, in this proscribed tattered village plank cottage in which I'm lavishing in anguish in the coarse village ghetto. I craved to comprehend better the reason for his saying that. Perceiving the startle on my face,

He continued…

*Quote... *if my priority was to be praised, I wouldn't have come to existence, because none existed then...*

From here, I got it better. Then this word plunged in my mind...

Quote... It's your motives that will give you the platform to be seen...

Then I noticed that it was the incessant impulse to have a better life that equestrian my assiduous stay in the rejected old village plank cottage, on the precluded antiquated putrid dual pew sofa. From there, my cognizance elongated on motives. My wits began giving supplementary messages. My cravings then were to see others elated and fulfilled, however from a horrid ghetto.

Then my tutor said...

"You can only fight to defend what you love. Love gives you strength from within to confront all challenges. A lady once said "I don't love singing, but gifted in singing as a singer.".…

…Sequence yourself to love what you're skilled in. Train yourself to love your star, your star needs your love. You can't thrive with your star if you cannot love it. Love what you were meant to do. Life isn't a fluke, but veracity. Anything you love, takes your time." He told me.

My senses were in person standing next to me, as he communicated sense in me. I heeded, as he spoke in plain words. Then I asked this question. "What's the need of my star in my ghetto?" the question.

He said…

"Your star is naught devoid of your ghetto. The need of your star in your ghetto is vital. You may not excel, if you don't understand the need of your star in your ghetto. Stars are needed ghettoes because hopes are needed in the ghettoes…

Quote… Your star is needed in your ghetto, because her presence eradicates frustration, and implant hopes, for a better future…

Then I probed the subsequent query, as he paced handier in me. "How can I ascertain the need of my star in my ghetto?" I asked.

He said…

"There're copious ways in which one can ascertain the need of a star in a ghetto…

Trace a Need.

You need to be able to trace the need in the ghetto first. What's needed in this locality in which I'm going, and how can I aid that forth? Not answering this is the inability to aid out issues. Know what the people want, and how you can help them out. Discovering a need is the key secret on how to help the ghetto. If you can't trace a need, then you won't be traced in the help…

Know your Stand.

A bloke left his house prompt at dawn, and stood by the kerb. Watching others as they pass to their various jobsites. As he observed, he saw an attorney roll in a clean car, well garbed and he venerated the barrister, concluding in him to become a lawyer. As he mused, he saw a surgeon roll pass in an ample archetypal car than that of the attorney, he still valued and pledged himself to someday become a physician. As he was talking, he saw a journalist rolled in a more prototypical jeep, than that of the advocate and the specialist, and he did the same…

…And the day ended, without him rallying anything to pageant forth from the day's approbation. He never stood on one aspect to have a stand in life. You need to know your stand, for that's what will upkeep you. Know what you are living for, and halt hopping from one mind-set to another.

Be Ardent.

Devoid of craving, one may not do what he aspires. The paramount is the Concern about the welfare of those you aspire to aid. There're folks that you may not get the motives of their cries if you can't cry along. Your craving needs to drive you. Be move with what moves those you intent to succor. Without passion in your dreams you may die dreaming.

Circumvent Pride.

It can rescind a life and fate. You shouldn't go up in life, you should grow…

Quote… It's better to take a long road and succeed with time, than to take a short road and die in time…

Quote… Pride kills your talent in time, while humility grows your talent with time…

Quote… The paraphernalia to your dream and quest of helping the ghetto is in your approach towards humility…

I was more concern on how to do it in my ghetto. I needed more teachings on what one can do to become a star in a ghetto. I was much fascinated on that. "How can I execute the need of my star in my ghetto?" I asked.

He unremitted…

"Recognizing the need of a star in a ghetto is one thing, and the way to execute the need of a star in a ghetto is still another thing…

Set Goals.

Set goals on how you anticipate to implement the need of your star, by delineating the various necessities in altered constituencies beneath your assessment. Have aims as your remit. A chaotic person cannot amalgamate others. Botch of goals you will be drudging not seeing the expanse enclosed. Goals always speak in the future of a vision. A timeframe for a works is very important.

Have a Vision.

Visualize after setting goals. One may not meet the needs in the ghetto devoid of a flawless vision. Constructing goals, swerve it into a vision. Vision, a written plan of move comprising goals. Chat of your triumph as a star in your ghetto, with the future in mind …"

Quote… Vision is the key to anyone with a future. Anyone that has a future walks with a vision. 'A life with no vision is a life with no future.' …

One of the stars intervallic by saying…

*Quote… *I'm a star to many today, and viewed by all because I existed when there was none to watch and praise me then, but I had the mind-set that one day, I will be viewed and praised by all, which is now…*

Then my teacher continued…

"…Let your assessment of the future dome your today. The ghetto has to do with a vision on those you anticipate aiding…

Have a Scheme.

…A project as the preliminary point towards aiding those in the ghetto. Once a need is pinpointed, scheme a means of aid through a venture. Folks follow once there's something to grasp, perceive, touch, feel and benefit from, they'll acquiesce to the mentorship effusively. The credence is inculcated through what one can see, feel, touch, hear and benefit from. Conserved protocol is an extinct expanse in time. It's easy to become a star in your ghetto. Your goal should be your global view…

Delegate those in the Ghetto.

For a feat in the ghetto as a star, delegation of those therein to aid in the work is germane. There're altered types of folks in the ghetto, comprising the educated. Include them so they can see their worth, finding some sense of fitting. Lone the mediocre to you will honor you in becoming a star. It's proficiency in the same arena that divulges superiority. Get them encompass in your pursuit of making their ghetto a better place, and your exertions will be grasped. Make them understand that they're not the coarsest category of people. Get them beneath your vision by service and doles.

Be a Leader…"

Then one of the stars intervened again, by saying…

Quote… *I'm praised on earth because my presence from here (sky, ghetto) is visible…

My tutor unremitted with the lessons. I loved it, as I craved auxiliary. I've already filled four block notes.

Here was what he said…

Quote… Stars are seen, though small in size. People can only make you trivial in scope, and you're the lone folk to trifle yourself in value…

"Just be the leader in the ghetto. The criterion of a leader is the oddity of a star.

Be Able to Feel.

Quote… If you can't feel, then you can't feed…

Quote… Affections drive intentions…

It's not the amount, but the type of gift that matters. It's not the type by value, but from the heart. An optimistic affection can vintage away an adverse intention. Let your fondness towards those in the ghetto be sanguine. Feel for them, in other to see their needs. The way you feel towards something or somebody, drives the way you act towards the same.

Loyalty.

Authenticity earns reliance and full staunchness. A star should be a man of his words at all times. A star barely speaks, reacts, and promises for their words are meant. Words depict the heart." He ended, as I faced the stars.

Taking a profound breath, he ended. I was transmogrified by all that he fathomed. I unambiguous to drill all that he'd said. I vouchsafed myself never to be a botch in any way. I'd nosedived to the level of having a sojourn amid torpors, grime, birds, beetles, and darkness. Eating the least category of the local traditional meal, and lining diurnally on an old dirty rejected reeking double seat couch in an old rejected village plank cottage, in a nation where none cares about the concerned necessitating cohort amid which I was one of them. That was indeed a gigantic botch. Despite all that, my thoughts went deeper.

"I will never fail in life!" I screeched audibly. Was I insane? Yeah. If aberration was the pacesetter, then I crave it for normality. That I did because of what I was able to swot. Obviously, with such astuteness, failure can only emanate through your acquiescence. As one of the stars heard me voice that aloud, he paced towards me and said…

*Quote… *I'm a star not by sound, but by actions. I'm seen and not heard, that's why I am attractive and not abstractive…*

From here I could notice that action counts for the paraphernalia of acumen to be seen, and not words of what one may know. Then another star, not far from where I stood spoke and said…

Quote… *though without a voice, all can still look at me, that's why I am a star…

Then my tutor asked me the ensuing, which instigated me to ruminate hard…

Quote… Can someone still see you in your hush and actions? Are you a talking type or an acting type? …

Then the stars unremitted…

Quote… *the sun doesn't just give oomph to me for free, but I enthrall verve to myself from the sun by actions…

Quote… *I understood that talking won't give me the capacity to be seen in this my little size, but actions that can draw attentions to me by causing people to wonder if I'm the one shining like this, was the solution…

Quote… *I knew that folks obviously must have been tired of sounds of thunder, rain, wind, seas, voices and birds, that's why I unequivocal to bring something new, because of human curiosity towards new things. That's why I selected sparkling and not the way of the multitude…

*Quote… *I'm single in sparkling. The sun shines, but I sparkle, that's why I'm a star…*

Forfeiting supplementary courtesy to my tutor, he spoke in lofty tunes through the veins schmoosing my wits cubicles. Trying to condense his memorandum, this was the memo…

Quote… If you can be seen, then you will be heard from others…

"Are your actions dazzlingly led as a star that you were created to be? A man's whereabouts publicizes him more than mere words. There is no career devoid of charisma. There's a character abode, and a linguistic of stars. Your star will shine and prevail in your ghetto if you trail the decorum of stars. Your ghetto needs you and your star, in other to venerate you into a star. Your absence from the ghetto is the deferral of your star shining on the surface. You can do it if in your ghetto." He said.

Then he taught me the four things that are required for an efficacious shining in my ghetto as a star.

"There're four stuffs you need for an optimistic lifetime feat in your ghetto reign as a star." He said, numerating…

Acumen! Fanaticism! Finance! Folks!

Be enthusiastic and in terrific ardor, to thrive in your ghetto as a star. A meager bloke is the disenfranchised in a ghetto. Any can acquiesce, once the need is perceived. Finance for your incessant halt at the top as a star is vital. Marshal your pecuniary dispositions, in view to kick-off in your ghetto towards becoming a star.

You need quality and not multitude of folks in your ghetto. Devoid of people, you can't reign as a star. You need others in your ghetto, in other to be clapped. No servant, no lordship.

A star is like a present that is sent to a man, and he has been there for decades in woe, while the gift was proposed to culminate travail. Because he never took note of it, he remained in misery as the present loitered."…

Quote… The timing is at your control. The day you discover, that day you start exhibiting…

Its 3a.m. My cognizance screeched as I got up, fast, from my terrace. I've spent the night outside. Places are calm and quiet. You have to go and rest, I told myself. I was indeed tired.

EIGHT

SHINING IN YOUR GHETTO

The next day!

Sited on my old dirty rejected reeking tattered double seat couch, in the old rejected disseminated village plank cottage. How am I going to start all of this? My cognizance probed. Inapt in thoughts, I rifled my sanities.

Then my tutor started…

"He'd let me divulge some cavernous things to you."
He said. "For your star to be maintained there're things
you need and those you don't. I will start with those
you don't need." He unremitted. "Here's the common
acumen and opines of men." He told me, as he
continued…

"Nemeses of efficacious shining in the ghetto.

Who're those things that stands as the adversaries of
an efficacious shining in the ghetto?

a- Malevolent Comrades.

They're the paramount sort you should evade in your
ghetto in other to marmalade your star' brilliance. This
type has the capacity to deter you from enjoying the
perks in your ghetto.

1- Who are Comrades?

Mobile buddies.

They can cavalcade you to anywhere you anticipate a
walk with one to. They're constantly with you on your
indolent hours. These categories are seen with you
ubiquitously. They have access to your confidentiality.

One You Segment Your Enigmas With.

These ones can be dawdling and modest in
assassinating progressively. You may not see them as
unscrupulous, for they can be good eavesdroppers and

deliberate in speech. Be cautious with the one you confine the enigmas to, despite how handy they are.

Deputies.

We never can tell, be alert. Not all assistants are publicists of vision. If you're told the factual dye of the devil, I qualm if you will believe. Don't ruminate all as seraphs. Your nemeses can be your assistants (P.As.) one can't say, but time always tells. Anyone who plays best, last at last.

Play pals.

One can be cavorting to an abode of compunctions in life. Those you play with tallies. They delineate your scene in life. Frolicking with a youngster and finding yourself on the ground should be the probable. Frisking with a smoker and inhaling the smoke of cigarettes is the plausible. Romping with water and being wet is the viable. Gamboling with an infantile and dialoguing childishly in other to flow in line is the doable. The sun doesn't frolic with the stars, though in the same sky. This isn't smugness, but a state of mind that sets one above.

Mentors.

Not all advisers are good ones. You may never be yonder your perpetual adviser. Your mentors are your controllers, even when you're not hiking in line their counsel. It lays something in your awareness. Flawless their directions might seem. A good guidance is not known by the way it's offered, but from whom it comes, and the motives. Why benevolent me this counsel? Is the veracious question. Reasons are request, which is why the mind is, 'power in store'." He taught.

All of this infiltrated my all, as I tacit how I can fanfare in my ghetto and my stay maintained as a star.

He continued…

b- The Proud.

They can effortlessly bait stimulus from your cohorts, to their malevolent habits. They love chatting about themselves to the debasing of others. A proud man always sees himself afar his confines not divulging the actualities about their incapacities. A proud man is a snare to a good leader. Ample auxiliary stuffs emanate conceit on folks.

c-   Vision Assassins.

Vision killers, they've the propensity from within to assassinate a vision. At this interval…

The Indolent.

Any who can't drudge in a vision can annihilate it through languor. These are those who love whines.

They clasp motives for each fault committed by them. To a languorous man, a day inaugurates with a groan, and culminates with a grin. The visit of the assessor shouldn't be today so that I can cope to put stuffs unruffled. He always anticipates for a tomorrow that never stems.

The Antagonists.

They opposes at all-time, even when there's no need to. They would always want their rash ideas to be implemented. They'll try to monogram anything they say to suit them, in view for notice.

d- The Lazy.

There's never a habitation devoid of the indolent. Languorous folks are threat to your reign in your ghetto as a star. They're good politicians with mouth purpose. This type places sentiments before reasons.

e-   Faultfinders.

This type whines at everything. Noble and cruel. They whinge, not looking for an accelerative lane. If you don't have an insinuation about a matter, then let thinkers propose and halt complaining. There's no reason grouchy without a proposition. They've naught to pageant forth for an advancement in the ghetto.

…I will continue with you soon, time to meet the stars." He told me, perceiving the occurrence of the stars. He was sympathetic.

Pacing out, I unambiguous to take a hike around. Fascinated on the sky, I was elated by the star. Inaudibly, I stood adjacent to the star. Obviously, all my probes were elucidated. I just needed to become a star. I already knew how to conserve my shining as a star. Staring at him, I noticed myself reasoning and inaugurating shrugs like one of them, I was a star.

Inaudible, as they were, for I was already one of them. Was it probable? What's the unfeasibility in it? Then, one of the stars ruptured the hush. He was happy as I saw. He relished the dark, using it as an advantage.

And here he said…

Quote… *One of the reasons why I love shining in the dark is because, there I have no worry, and everyone minds their business…

He chuckled, as my sanities grinned gazing at his wisdom, acutely. Galvanized by it, I stood ready and avid to hear more.

He continued, amused. I relished it as he spoke…

Quote… *why should I complain about the performance of my colleague? His weakness and strength is an opportunity for me to be seen among…

Then I traumatized my hush with a chuckle. It was deep indeed, but hilarious above all. Then the other said, detecting my laughter…

*Quote… *why should I complain about how bright my friend shines? His brightness will draw more attention up the sky, and I will be notice among…*

*Quote… *the glory of my fellow star is an advantage to me…*

Then I inaugurated reasons cantankerous with none, including myself. Understanding the need for unity, I saw life as a sacrosanct combat of preference that should be void of pressure. I've tacit that pressure and drudgery is not what makes it, but the pleasure you derive from doing the right thing.

Life to me was a battle that should be wrestled in elation and contentment. Peace of mind was one of the weapons necessary for the conquest of the combat, called life. Defeatism, remorse, and low self-esteem became a lethal antagonist to the fight. I realized that clemency is a diurnal cypher that petrifies the adversary and wanes his craws.

Positivity in speech and acts was my forte as I was audacious to face life. She was a gift that was to be celebrated diurnally and never to be bemoaned. I could see gaffes as mentors; assign to role me through life. Time and age was an extra subsidy from life. Work was an exercise of comfort given by life, which should be cherished and not eluded. I laughed, seeing my ghetto, a place to be in which I belong.

I could sense everything in me, though having naught in my account. Was there any account? How I wish I had one. The feelings of indulgences unremitted, my tutor whispered in me, that there was a lot to know about my shining in the ghetto. Then he continued with those who're not needed in my life, for my continual brilliance therein…

f-   The Wiseacre.

"One can never be boss on everything, unless the vision is ruled by triers of entirety. They claim to know this today, and that tomorrow. They're doing everything but naught to pageant. Important people have fix pedigrees. Any with no location is omitted. No address, no site. Your location is where you're found, and can be sketched. Until one is able to settle down, he may never grow. The strength of any growth is roots, roots are gained when engrained. Cuddle what you can do in your ghetto.

g- The Stupid.

Absurdity, a state of the mind that affects actions deleteriously. They do things before reasoning. Stupid people never understand things the way they should.

A stupid man can effortlessly disremember the past syrupy jiffies, because of a little contemporaneous acrimonious jiffy. An indiscreet man will not comprehend that 'his boss haven't paid him this month because he hasn't enough money, as he has said,' he resigns.

He folds the arms and whines about the pecuniary crunches, and not does anything that would aid out situations.

A stupid man prefers to drudge for the present forgetting the future, which will never halt staring in our eyes constantly.

An imprudent man would say, 'God for us all, everyone for himself. Better we eat; after all, we'll die.' He lives on what he sees, and flouts the coercions of the future that's never gloomed from staring at us face-to-face. He repulses reprimand. He loves applauds even when he is in the folly of his livid gaffes. He abhors it, when he's inspected. He finds no idiocy in his futility. Such are the nemeses of your star in the ghetto." He said. Disbursing supplementary courtesy to his instructions,

He continued, "These are not people you see." He said, leaving me in a mental pandemonium. I couldn't understand anything at all. Waiting for him to elucidate me, I maintained hush. Then he said, "No other person can carry any of these qualities apart for you." He inaugurated the raft, as my lips fell open.

What was he saying? I quizzed myself. "In you, all this allures are hidden." He told me. Then from here, I could interpret all the quotes from the stars. The eyes of my brain were extensively vulnerable, as I could see the reminiscence of everything and the discussions I've had with each stars. Revolving towards him,

He said, "None is wicked or malevolent, and there's none devoid of a kernel of tomfoolery." I could grasp all he said. Obviously, it's our scrutiny that takes others wicked and malign to us. What anyone does is to him. I could see that I was the lone who can enmesh me. None could, with such gen.

All Homo sapiens to me then weren't nemeses or imps. "That's the lone mind-set that can coalesce the world." He told me, grinning. Then a star paced handier and said, with his colleagues…

*Quote... *for me to start shining was an enigmatic, and for me to keep shining is still another mystery…*

*Quote... *for me to start shining I needed to be created and for me to keep shining I needed to stay close to the sun…*

*Quote... *I know the things I need, and the things I don't need in other to keep shining…*

*Quote... *it's not all that easy to shine in the dark (ghetto) in your mini size, though traumatic, but thanks to the etiquette that leads to braininess...*

*Quote... *what I do is that I sequence myself to kowtow in the decorum and that's why I'm still seen as a star. My oomph is the sun through tameness...*

*Quote... *I'm trivial to be grasped on earth because of the distance and my size, but I have all the enigmas from the sun...*

Then my tutor spoke in me and said…

a- Stay Optimistic.

"Stay sanguine on how you saw the whole thing from the on-set. Be buoyant in your ghetto even if the outcome in the beginning is tough, change-not…

b- Drudgery.

…Frail hands invite dearth and botch. Anything that made you into something can keep you into that thing. Hard work makes a man into a star, and lone maintains a star. Stars are never old because their exertions are always new.

Quote... Lone an indolent will whine on how rigid the drudgery was yesterday that he didn't work today...

c-   Ingenious.

The stars also spoke forth. I was entrenched through their words in my pursuit of becoming a star in my ghetto. I was already a star that hankered the prospect to shallow in the physical, which was just in less than an hour.

Then the stars said…

*Quote… *there're moments we come out heterogeneously in the sky, in big and small sizes because we have learned to be creative…*

*Quote… *today I can shine at the left side of the sky, big, and tomorrow I still shine in the other side of the sky, small…*

Quote… Creativity grosses longevity. Your feat span can be elongated by your creative ability…

Returning back in me, I knew that this was the last day, for I knew all that's required for my triumph in the ghetto. I wouldn't become the enemy to myself. Then my tutor rounded up with the teachings by telling me the following…

d- Unearthing.

"Disinterring is part of erudition with particulars. You need to key into knowing more about folks and kits. A bolt wits is a quasi- erudite. None knows all, but one can in the impulse for ample. That you don't know doesn't mean you can't. Your pursuit for unearthing will ascertain your proficiency in savvy matters. Endeavour with nostalgia to ascertain copious schemes of stuffs amid your ghetto environs.

Failure for auxiliary knowledge of your dwelling place debilitates exploration. Ample findings marmalades one in feat. Endeavour for ample actualities regarding other ghettoes, then you'll remain a star in yours. Sundry are wrecked today because they turn to contravene the knowledge that emanates from discovery.

Quote... If you can't discover, then you won't be discovered...

Quote... Anyone that strives to discover, is never covered because he always uncovers...

Then the star who introduced me the first day said, "Round up because after today you might not be jammy to have a chat with any of us." He said. But I knew they were going to stay perpetually in me.

The encounter was a profound and fascinating one that none would afford to miss. But one thing kept me gratified, he'd earlier told me that I was unrestricted to ask any question I wish, and each time I wanted. That alone kept me happy. At least, I was free to visit them at any time.

I had to return, the world needed me. I had to round up my search, for they were soon going to stop shining. My chaperon had told me that he was going to tell me the reason why they don't shine in all seasons, that was to be by next season. I will put it down in the volume two.

The other stars hastened towards me for their last words. They were going to miss me, big time. Then I jotted it down, while on my way to the earth. I was returning with a mind-set of change.

Here, their last words…

Union!

*Quote… *the sky is more attractive during our shining moments because we shine in a group as individuals…*

*Quote… *we noticed that union brings force to individual skills on how to shine and brighten the sky (ghetto) in their various spaces…*

*Quote… *I am not attractive enough without the presence of my fellow colleagues…*

Then my tutor talked to me as I returned, happy and fulfilled, ready for alteration in view of my dirty old rejected smelling couch, in the dirty old rejected village plank cottage of an abandoned uncivilized dirty village, in a corrupted satanic evil unemployment country, as such. I was indeed ready to change my world.

Here, the last words of my tutor…

"Hiking in union is a benefit to each star in the sky (ghetto). Stars need each other in other to unleash their personal know-how. You may not shine to the amusement of others, if not amongst. Stop trying to separate yourself. Unity brings power to individual skills." He said. It was also his last words…

Epilogue

The encounter with my mind and the stars from my veranda brought about an immense alteration in me, as I will forever benefit from. Am ready now to change my world (ghetto). In the second part of this book, I am going to divulge how I have used my experience and lessons from the stars in my world, and the benefits.

Behold the universe of thought…

All of this happened while from my veranda, in front of my old rejected village plank cottage, as I lay on my old dirty rejected smelling double seat couch, staring at my old cobwebbed roof. The old dirty rejected smelling double seat couch was the lone asset I had.

It was a mental life changing thoughts I had during my mission trip, while in the southwest region, Cameroon. It has nothing to do with spirits, demons, angels, and the world of the spirits. Neither the practices, but inspirations not distant from the author's understanding.

The voyage took several months, not precise, but here at the end. Oh, my beloved tutor, the mind…

YOU CAN FOLLOW NE ON:

Facebook:

NOVELIST VESOH.

**CAMEROON YOUNG WRITERS
PLATFORM**

Instagram:

NOVELIST RENE

Twitter:

NOVELIST VESOH

Whattsapp:

(+237 678938471)